Parabulz

Andrew Bianchi

Illustrated by Andy Gray

PARABULZ

Copyright © Andrew Bianchi 2006
First published 2006
ISBN 978 1 84427 227 3

Scripture Union, 207–209 Queensway, Bletchley, Milton Keynes, MK2 2EB, England.
Email: info@scriptureunion.org.uk
Website: www.scriptureunion.org.uk

Scripture Union Australia
Locked Bag 2, Central Coast Business Centre, NSW 2252
Website: www.scriptureunion.org.au

Scripture Union USA
PO Box 987, Valley Forge, PA 19482
Website: www.scriptureunion.org

The right of Andrew Bianchi to be identified as author of this work has been asserted by him in accordance with the Copyright, Designs and Patents Act 1988.

Andy Gray has asserted his right under the Copyright, Designs and Patents Act 1988, to be identified as illustrator of this work.

British Library Cataloguing-in-Publication Data.
A catalogue record of this book is available from the British Library.

Printed and bound in Malta by Progress Print

Cover design by four-nine-zero design

Typesetting and layout by Creative Pages, www.creativepages.co.uk

Scripture Union is an international Christian charity working with churches in more than 130 countries, providing resources to bring the good news about Jesus Christ to children, young people and families and to encourage them to develop spiritually through the Bible and prayer.

As well as our network of volunteers, staff and associates who run holidays, church-based events and school Christian groups, we produce a wide range of publications and support those who use our resources through training programmes.

Contents

		PAGE
1.	To begin with...	7
2.	Sow what?	12
3.	It's a bit like...	21
4.	Gotcha!	33
5.	What are you like?	45
6.	OT Gotchas	64
7.	OT parabulz	72
8.	Ready for Jesus	83
9.	What's God like?	95
10.	Mainly about Jesus	103

1. To begin with...

That particular day had begun like all the other Fridays he could remember. Everything was the same – the sounds, the sights, the same people bustling past his window – racing to nowhere and then back again. Just another Friday.

The steps were still there. They'd always been there. Beckoning. Inviting. If steps could talk – and who is to say these couldn't? – they might even have called out, "Come on. Down you come."

So that Friday afternoon, although the morning had been like all the others, he did what those steps wanted. He listened. And before he knew it he was standing on the first stair, then the second. Now he could no longer see the old piano, stiff and rigid in the fading light. Down he went,

deeper and deeper into the mysterious hole in the ground... past the shelves of fading music and row after row of books... down, down... until he stopped, facing a large square object. A picture of a beautiful woman hung to one side. He stared in wonder at her image.

To one side, on a desk covered in papers, lay a series

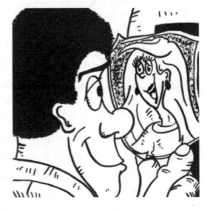

of letters – in a pattern that reminded him of a half-learned lesson or an easily forgotten rhyme. Above them hovered 15 guardians, threatening and brooding. The man hesitated as he looked at them, and steeled his mind. Then, almost instinctively, he leaned forward and pressed a button. Without thinking, he eased himself onto a dark brown chair that wobbled and swayed as he sunk into it. Lights flashed and a gentle whine broke the eerie silence. He grew excited and his fingers began to run over the letters. Hitting this one, missing that. Faster and faster, until his hand hammered down one last time and he slumped back.

There was nothing left to do. He had done all he could. He would have to wait. Only time would tell whether that particular Friday really was just the same as all the others...

OR TO PUT IT ANOTHER WAY...

On Friday 22 April 2005, having been tinkering tunelessly away on the piano, I finally went into my study, which is in the cellar of my house. By my desk, and slightly to the right, there is a picture of the players in my rugby team. I shuddered at the sight of myself and resolved to lose weight for the start of next season. I sat down and switched on the computer (where a picture of my wife is stuck onto the side of the screen with Blu-tack) and sent an email to those wonderful (their words, not mine) people at Scripture Union. In the email was an idea for a follow-up book to *10 Rulz*. (What do you mean, you've never seen it? Stop reading immediately and go and buy a copy!)

AVAILABLE FROM ALL GOOD CHRISTIAN BOOKSHOPS OR FROM SU MAIL ORDER — SEE PAGE 110 FOR DETAILS.

Do you like reading or listening to a good story? You're not alone! With the possible exception of the boffs in your class, everybody likes a story. Stories are so much more fun than dull facts. Stories make us laugh, cry, feel frightened, nervous, angry or curious. And what can facts do? Turn us into nerds! Even teachers realise the power of stories and they will often trick you into learning things by using them. Just when you thought you were having fun – wham! You've understood some bit of history or geography.

Using stories to teach things is not a new idea. People have used them for ages to explain tricky ideas. Not only can they help us understand important stuff, but they are easier to remember too.

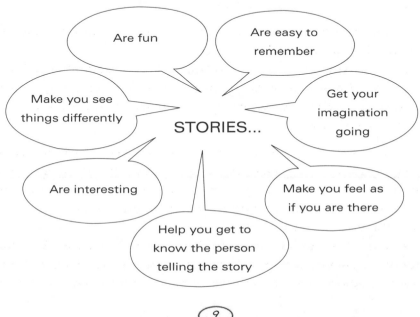

PARABULZ

In the Bible there are lots of stories with a special name. Parables. Or if you want to spell them badly – Parabulz.

Most of them were told by Jesus, but there are others as well. Read them. Enjoy them... but don't blame me if you learn at the same time!

I SAID *PARABULZ*, NOT A *PAIR OF BULLS*

As you go through this book you'll discover that I've split it up into chapters. There were two reasons for this.

1 People usually split up books into chapters, so I thought I'd better do the same.
2 I knew it would be a lot of fun thinking up stupid titles for each chapter. The downside of chapters is that once you've got them, you have to work out which parable belongs in which one. It's not an easy task.

I don't know if you've ever tried eating a spaghetti sandwich. It's very messy. As soon as you have it ready a bit dangles out one side, and if you push it back in then another strand pops out somewhere else. Italians who make spaghetti know it's a pretty stupid thing to do, so they don't even try.

As I was working out where to put some of the parables, I often thought I'd packed one in the right chapter only to discover that a bit was hanging over into another one. So if you see one and think

it's in the wrong place, don't worry – the chances are you may be right. If Jesus had wanted his parables to be in neat and tidy chapters, I'm sure he could have arranged it. But he didn't, so I suppose it doesn't really matter after all.

2. Sow what?

One of the most famous parables Jesus told was about a man who sowed some seed. It's famous for two reasons. First of all, you can read about it in three of the Gospels, which means that each of the authors must have thought it was pretty important. Also, Jesus says some unusual things about why he decided to talk in parables. But more of that later...

Jesus had left the house to have a quiet sit-down by the side of the lake. (It's always drier to sit down at the side of a lake than in the middle of it!) But as so often happened, it turned out to be anything but quiet. Huge numbers of people crowded round to see him. Jesus decided there were too many people, so he got into a boat – probably so he wouldn't be squashed. He sat down straight away and started to speak.

One man went to sow

One day a farmer collected a large, heavy bag. Inside it were hundreds and thousands of tiny seeds. He marched off to his field and began the job of planting seeds. Instead of digging a hole for each individual grain, he shoved his hand deep into the bag and pulled out a handful at a time. Then, remembering where he had started, and aiming towards a tree at the other end of the field, he began throwing the seed away from himself. Hand in. Grab. Scatter. Hand in. Grab. Scatter. Hand in. Grab. Scatter. All day long that's what he did. Walking up in a straight line then turning to one side, taking a few steps and going back in the other direction. The bag got lighter and lighter until eventually it was empty. All the seed had gone.

But gone where?

Some of the seed had landed on the hard, dry path that ran around the edges of the field. As it did so, crafty birds that had been watching the man flew down and gobbled up anything they could find.

Other grain had landed on parts of the field that were covered in stones and rocks. A short while later, little green shoots could be seen peeping above the soil. All seemed to be going well but because of the stones there wasn't much soil, and the plants couldn't put down very deep roots to suck up the moisture. So when the summer sun was at its hottest, the plants dehydrated and began to flop over and turn a yellowy-brown colour.

Some of the seed sailed through the air and landed among some little plants. This was a problem because these plants would grow to be prickly thorn bushes. The grain and the thorns grew up together and both seemed to be getting along fine, but the thorns grew more quickly and were stronger than the other seeds, so they took all the goodness from the soil and stretched out to absorb the sun's rays. The farmer's seed never stood a chance and was choked to death.

But lots of the seed landed in good soil. Through the seasons of rain and sunshine it grew steadily. At harvest time there was a fantastic crop. Tens of hundreds of plants were produced from the amount of seed that had been sown.

Matthew 13:1-23,
Mark 4:1-20
and Luke 8:4-15

FACTS

IN BIBLE TIMES, FARMERS SOWED THEIR CROPS IN OCTOBER AND NOVEMBER — THE TIME OF THE YEAR WHEN THERE WOULD BE LOTS OF RAIN AFTER THE HOT, DRY SUMMER.

Any ideas what that parable is all about? If you think you know, then you're better than Jesus' followers. They hadn't a clue what he was talking about. So Jesus told them the code to crack it. See if you can use the codecracker to crack Jesus' coded message on the next page!

PARABULZ

A	B	C	D	E	F	G	H	I	J	K	L	M	N	O	P	Q	R	S	T	U	V	W	X	Y	Z
25	23	21	19	17	15	13	11	9	7	5	3	1	2	4	6	8	10	12	14	16	18	20	22	24	26

The seed: 20 4 10 19   4 15   13 4 19

The seed falling on the path: 14 11 4 12 17   20 11 4   11 17 25 10   23 16 14
19 4 2 14   23 17 3 9 17 18 17

The seed falling on the rocks: 14 11 4 12 17   20 11 4   11 17 25 10   23 16 14
13 9 18 17   16 6

The seed falling in the thorns: 14 11 4 12 17   20 11 4   11 17 25 10
23 16 14   19 4 2 14   13 10 4 20

The seed falling on good soil: 14 11 4 12 17   20 11 4   11 17 25 10   25 2 19
5 17 17 6   13 4 9 2 13

FACTS

IN SPORTS TOURNAMENTS, TEAMS OR INDIVIDUAL PLAYERS ARE OFTEN SEEDED (OR RANKED) IN ORDER. THIS IS A KIND OF FIX TO TRY TO MAKE SURE A CROP OF EXCITING MATCHES COMES TOWARDS THE END OF THE COMPETITION.

Just in case you still haven't worked out, let's see what Jesus himself said about the parable.

The first thing to remember is that the seed stands for God's Word. Remember that and it all begins to make sense.

The seeds that fall on the path are like people who hear God's Word. But God's enemy, the devil, comes along and snatches it away from their minds. In this way they can't trust in the message and be rescued by what it says.

The seeds that fall on the rocky area are like people who hear God's Word and get really excited about it. But there is no real depth to the way they feel about it. They think it's OK for a while, but when something tricky comes along they give up completely.

The seeds that fall among the prickly thorns are like people who hear God's Word but they spend so much time doing all kinds of stuff that they never seem to have time to think seriously about what God wants. So they never make any progress.

The seeds that fall on the good soil are like people who hear God's Word and allow it to affect everything that they do. Their lives end up producing lots of kind deeds and actions that show they do what God wants.

In each case, the seed is the same. It is just where it lands, that changes. If you had to put yourself in one of those types of soil, which one would it be? Why?

One of the odd things about this story is its name. Most people call it the parable of the sower. But I think really it should be called the parable of the soils. After all, they are the interesting bit in this parable. Do you think I'm right? Or am I crazy? (Please only answer the first question.)

Now, that parable is good enough and challenging enough on its own, but I also said that it would give us a clue as to why Jesus said lots of things using parables. Not only did his disciples ask him what this particular parable was all about, they asked him another question too. They wanted to know why he spoke in parables so much of the time.

Jesus' reply was pretty interesting. He didn't say, "Because everyone likes a good story." Nor did he say, "It makes what I am saying easier to remember." Instead his reply was even trickier to understand than most of his parables!

It goes something like this.

Jesus said that what he was teaching was secret stuff. Normally when we think of secrets we think of codes, mysteries or what our best friend has made us promise not to tell anyone else – like who they fancy, or the fact their teddy stays in bed with them. But when Jesus talked about secrets he meant things that were only hidden because people didn't look hard enough for them or just did not want to understand.

Secrets about the author

WHICH ONE OF THESE IS A SHAMEFUL SECRET ABOUT THE AUTHOR?

- [ ] HIS FAVOURITE FOOTBALL TEAM IS BRIGHTON AND HOVE ALBION
- [ ] HE ONCE CAME 26TH OUT OF 25 IN AN EXAM AT SCHOOL
- [ ] HE SHAVES USING JUST A RAZOR AND WATER
- [ ] HE ONCE WENT TO A HISTORY LESSON WEARING JUST HIS SWIMMING TRUNKS

The answer is that all of them are true. You can decide whether they are shameful or not. It's like when we can't find our trainers or our mobile phone. What happens? If we've got any sense, we go to

PARABULZ

Mum or Dad (or Gran or Uncle Bill or whoever cares for us). Normally they say, "Have you looked for it?" We say, "No." And that explains why we haven't found it. Then off they go and two seconds later they come back with a scowl, holding the offending object.

God's secrets aren't really secrets at all – any more than our trainers were hidden. They are simply things that people have never really bothered to think about or tried to discover.

This secret stuff of Jesus was what Jesus was giving to his friends in parable form. He was handing it to them because God wanted them to know and understand what was what. These friends were interested in finding out about God – that was why they were with Jesus. And all the stories and parables he was telling them made them even more curious to find out more.

When someone who wasn't really interested in finding out about God heard a parable, they just shrugged their shoulders and said it didn't make much sense. They couldn't be bothered to make

This is brilliant!

the effort to try to find out more, because they just weren't fussed. They could hear and listen all right, but they weren't into understanding. (Why do I keep on thinking of maths when I write something like this?)

Parables were Jesus' way of making people sit up and think. If they decided they'd rather slouch down again and not

pay any notice then it was really just a sign that they didn't want to know about God in the first place. But if they were interested, or just curious, they'd try to find out more. Just like what Jesus' friends did when they asked him about it in the first place.

And now to the rest of this book! There's plenty more where that parable came from – more than 35, but it's easy to lose count!

3. It's a bit like...

Imagine your maths teacher comes into the class one day and says, "The answer to 10 plus 5 is roughly somewhere between, oh, I don't know, say 13 and 21." You'd think a couple of things.

You'd be disappointed that they'd turned up at all and you didn't have a chance to do something useful instead, like talking to your friends or reading a good book.

You'd think they were being a bit vague – not the way a maths teacher normally behaves. (The one thing you wouldn't think is that the teacher had gone mad. Everyone knows maths teachers are pretty crazy already.)

We expect teachers to be specific – to give exact answers. But when Jesus told a parable he wasn't always like that. You might have expected him to be precise, to give exact details to everything. Instead, sometimes he was, well, a bit vague...

Look, for example, at what he said God's kingdom was like...

We'd better weed, hadn't we?

The farmer decided to go and plant some wheat in his freshly ploughed field. He chose the very best seed he could find and set about sowing it evenly, right across the rich, fertile soil. By the end of the day he was exhausted, but happy too, as the field had all been covered with the tiny seed. But while he was fast asleep in bed, his enemy came along. He too had seed ready to sow. They weren't wheat seeds, though. His seed came from horrible weeds. All night he sowed, quietly and sneakily.

When the first rays of light stretched out across the field he disappeared, leaving the scene as if nothing had happened.

Later on, as the young shoots began to squeeze their way up through the soil, the farmer's servants noticed that something was not quite right. They couldn't just see ears of healthy corn. All manner of nasty weeds were shooting up too, using up the goodness of the earth. They rushed to their boss.

"Sir, something weird has happened to your wheat field! You sowed good seed, didn't you? But the field is covered in weeds. What on earth has happened?"

The farmer realised that someone else must have done something. There were just too many weeds for it to have happened by chance. "One of my enemies must have done this," he sighed.

"What shall we do then?" his servants asked. "Do you want us to go and sort him out?"

(That last speech isn't in the story, but I thought it sounded like the kind of thing a keen servant, eager to impress, would say to his master. What they really said was...)

"Shall we go and pull the weeds up now?"

"No," came the reply. "Wait. If you attack the weeds now you'll probably wrench out some of the wheat as well. Leave things as they are. When it's harvest time I'll have a word with the harvesters. They can tie up the weeds into bundles and then chuck them on a fire. The good wheat that remains can be placed in my barn for storage."

Matthew 13: 24–30,36–43

Now, Jesus' followers weren't quite sure what the point of the story was. So they asked Jesus to explain what he meant. And he did.

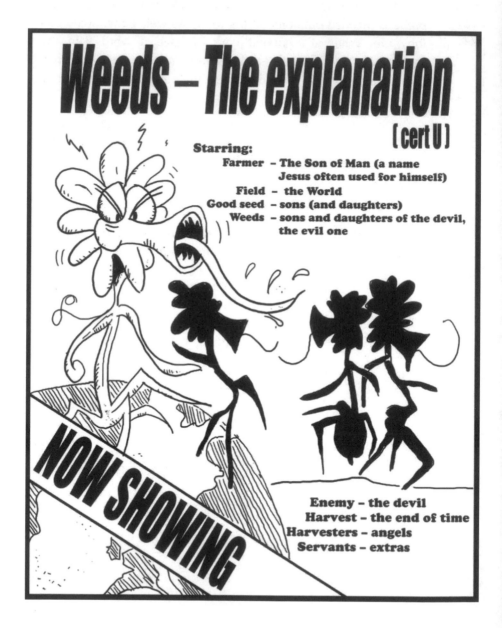

Weeds – The explanation
(cert U)

Starring:

Farmer – The Son of Man (a name Jesus often used for himself)

Field – the World

Good seed – sons (and daughters)

Weeds – sons and daughters of the devil, the evil one

NOW SHOWING

Enemy – the devil

Harvest – the end of time

Harvesters – angels

Servants – extras

REVIEW OF *WEEDS – THE EXPLANATION*

FOLLOWING ON FROM JESUS' SUCCESSFUL PARABLE OF THE WEEDS, AUDIENCES WERE LEFT IN CONFUSION AS TO WHAT THE STORY WAS ALL ABOUT. ALL IS REVEALED IN *WEEDS – THE EXPLANATION*. IN THIS ACTION-PACKED PARABLE, JESUS CLEVERLY WEAVES SPIRITUAL TRUTHS TOGETHER WITH TRIED – AND TRUSTED – FARMING TECHNIQUES TO BRING A STUNNING CLIMAX TO ONE OF THE HOTTEST TOPICS OF ALL TIME: WHAT IS GOD'S KINGDOM REALLY LIKE?

THE ANSWER IS GIVEN IN ONE OF THE MOST SIMPLE YET SOBER ACCOUNTS OF THE END OF TIME. WITHOUT WANTING TO GIVE AWAY TOO MUCH OF THE PLOT, WE CAN REVEAL THAT JESUS HIMSELF WILL SEND HIS ANGELS TO WEED OUT ALL THOSE BAD THINGS AND PEOPLE THAT ARE THE CAUSE OF SO MUCH EVIL IN THE WORLD. THEY ARE THROWN INTO A TERRIBLE PLACE OF SADNESS AND SUFFERING. THE PEOPLE WHO HAVE TRUSTED GOD, ON THE OTHER HAND, ARE LEFT TO A DAZZLING FINALE IN THE VERY KINGDOM OF GOD HIMSELF.

NAME OF REVIEWER – FARMER GILES

WHAT OTHER REVIEWERS SAID...

Which are you? Weed or wheat?

The plot grew on me.

I'm glad I seed it.

PS Jesus finished the story by warning everyone who had ears to sit up and listen. (It might sound like a good pun – seeing as he'd been talking about ears of corn, but it only works in English. Not in Greek, the language in which the story was first written, or Aramaic, the language Jesus used most of the time).

It starts off small, I mustardmit

The kingdom of heaven is like

a mustard seed that someone plants. It is such a small seed and yet when it grows, it is the largest plant you'd expect to find in your garden. In fact, as a fully grown tree, it is so big that birds swoop down to perch in its branches.

yeast that someone might use in baking. If they take it and mix it into flour, it will work its way right through the dough.

And the point is: God's kingdom may not be too impressive to start with, but just you watch!

FACTS

THE CHINESE USED MUSTARD THOUSAND OF YEARS AGO. MUSTARD WAS ALSO USED BY ANCIENT GREEKS AND ROMANS AS A MEDICINE AND A SEASONING. IT SPREAD THROUGHOUT EUROPE AND INTO THE NEW WORLD. TODAY, MUSTARD COMES PRIMARILY FROM CANADA. MUSTARD'S HOT, SPICY FLAVOUR IMPROVES MEATS, FISH, FOWL, SAUCES AND SALAD DRESSINGS. WHOLE MUSTARD SEEDS ARE OFTEN USED IN PICKLING OR IN BOILING VEGETABLES SUCH AS CABBAGE. MUSTARD SEEDS ARE ALSO USED TO GIVE A NUTTY FLAVOUR TO INDIAN DISHES.

THE REAL NAME FOR YEAST IS *SACCHAROMYCES CEREVISIAE*, WHICH EXPLAINS WHY WE SIMPLY CALL IT YEAST! WHEN USED IN BREAD IT MAKES IT GROW LARGER (OR "RISE").

Hidden treasure

One day a man came across some treasure hidden in a field. As soon as he found it, what do you think he did? Of course. He hid it again so nobody else could find it – except himself. Then he raced away and sold off everything he owned. When the last car boot sale was over he took all the cash to the owner of the field and bought the field from him. At last the treasure was his!

Can you put these cartoons in the right order?

Pearl purchaser

It was Friday at the end of another busy week. Mr C Lam had been looking for pearls all over town. That was his job. He bought them and sold them, making as much money as he could along the way. It was hot and he was drinking with friends in a bar. Someone had just raised his glass and shouted out, "Oyster you," but C Lam wasn't listening. Across the street he saw a glint. His mussels tensed and he darted to where the flash came from. There in the shop window was the biggest pearl he'd ever seen in his life.

"What time do you close?", he asked the shopkeeper.

"In half an hour."

There wasn't much time. Lam rushed away to his neighbour, M O'llusc.

"Do you still want to buy my house?" he panted.

"I certainly do."

"Great. You can have everything inside it as well," replied Mr Lam.

"Well, you're certainly not shellfish," said his neighbour. He wrote out a cheque and Lam was off before the ink could dry. Twenty-nine minutes had passed. He'd made it.

At half past five, C Lam, collector of fine pearls, walked out of the shop with the biggest, most fantastic piece of jewellery he'd ever seen in his life.

How many dreadful bottom-of-the-sea puns can you find?

FACTS

PEARLS ARE MADE BY WATER-LIVING CREATURES CALLED MOLLUSCS — USUALLY OYSTERS. WHEN SOMETHING LIKE A GRAIN OF SAND GETS TRAPPED INSIDE THEM THEY COVER IT IN A CHEMICAL THAT EVENTUALLY FORMS A PEARL. GOOD ONES ARE WORTH A LOT OF MONEY.

TWO OLD WOMEN MEET AT A PARTY.
"MY DEAR," SAID THE FIRST WOMAN,
"ARE THOSE REAL PEARLS?"
"THEY ARE," REPLIED THE SECOND
WOMAN.
"OF COURSE, THE ONLY WAY I COULD
TELL WOULD BE FOR ME TO BITE THEM,"
SMILED THE FIRST.
"YES," SAID THE OTHER WOMAN, "BUT
FOR THAT YOU'D NEED REAL TEETH."

And the point is?

(a)   God's kingdom is so valuable that it's worth giving up
      everything to get it.

(b)   If you find something, you don't have to tell the police about it,
      but you can keep it for yourself.

(c)   It's not easy to write puns based on clams, oysters, molluscs,
      mussels and shellfish.

The answer is (a).   (b) is definitely wrong and if you think (c) is
wrong then have a go yourself and see what I mean.

Net result

Some of Jesus' followers were fishermen. What they didn't know
about fishing wasn't worth knowing. They didn't use a rod and
line like anglers do today. (It would take far too long to catch
enough fish to sell and make a living!) Instead they went out on
their local sea (called Galilee, or sometimes called Lake Tiberius) in
a boat, or they simply waded into the water with a large net. So it
made sense for Jesus to tell them stories like this one.

One day some fishermen let down their net into the water.
When they started to feel fish hitting the sides of the net, they knew
that it was full. Together they dragged it back to the shore, opened
it out and searched through everything that had got trapped inside.
One of them got a basket and they placed all the good tasty fish
that their customers liked inside, while they just got rid of the bad
fish, the weeds and bits of rubbish.

So now you're thinking, what has fishing got to do with God's kingdom? Should it be the kingdom of cod? Is there a plaice for everyone there? What happens to a person's sole? Will dreadful jokes be banned? To be honest, there wasn't a lot of information in the story, and Jesus' disciples were often not the brightest bunch in the world – so Jesus went on to explain what he meant. At the end of time, God will send angels to sort people. They will be like fishermen sorting out a catch of fish, keeping the good ones and throwing the bad ones away.

The clever thing about this story is that the fishermen not only understood it easily, but they said to themselves, "That makes sense. Nobody in their right mind is going to keep bad fish as well as good ones."

All these stories can be found in Matthew 13:24–52.

FACTS

CARP, SARDINES, MULLET AND CICHLID ARE ALL FOUND IN THE SEA OF GALILEE. THE CICHLID IS ALSO CALLED ST PETER'S FISH, AFTER JESUS' FRIEND, PETER.

Scattered seed succeeds in sprouting

Someone throws seed all over the ground. Then it begins to grow. All the time. Night and day. Whether the farmer is tucked up in bed or comes out to look at what he has planted. What's more, the farmer probably doesn't understand why it does! The soil simply makes the thing begin to grow until the stalk appears, then the ear and finally the whole grain in each ear is visible. When it is all ripe at harvest time, the farmer gets out a sharp sickle and cuts it down ready for his or her own use.

Mark 4:26-29

SICK or sick ee ?

So after all that, you may still be thinking: what exactly is the kingdom of God?

If you are, good! Remember that part of the point of a parable is to make you ask questions! The answer is both easy and difficult. The easy answer is that the kingdom of God is any place where God rules as king. (I told you it was easy.) The difficult part is working out exactly what that means. Someone's kingdom is usually where they are in charge, so God's kingdom can include any place, person or event where God is truly in charge.

4. Gotcha!

There's no doubt about it. Even his enemies would have to admit it. Even people who don't follow him today would agree with it. The fact is that Jesus was the nicest, kindest, gentlest person you could ever hope to meet. He wouldn't try to catch people out or make them look stupid in front of others. In fact, you might say he wouldn't say boo to a goose... or would he?

Actually, if you read the Bible closely, you'll see that Jesus *often* told stories to catch people out! Maybe not to make them look stupid, but to make them realise the way they thought or acted was not very good. In fact, some of his best-known parables could quite easily have finished with the word "Gotcha!"

I remember reading about a "Gotcha" done by some police in America. They had lost contact with some criminals and wanted to catch them. So they wrote letters to their last known addresses saying they had all won prizes in a competition. All the criminals had to do to claim their prize was to go to a certain building to collect them. When they got to that building, the police were waiting to arrest them! Gotcha!

Or, coming back to Jesus and what he said and did: "There. I've shown you up for bad attitude and petty ways of looking at things. You thought you'd be able to catch me out with your clever questions. Wrong! You think you know more about what God thinks than anyone else. Wrong again! In fact you're not even close. God thinks differently and he expects those who claim to follow him to think differently too. He's much bigger and kinder and more caring than you are, so you'd better change your ways."

"Gotcha!" is a much shorter way of putting things!

The ~~Good, Bad, Good, Bad~~ – oh you make up your own mind – Samaritan

"Jesus?" the top lawyer said.

"Yes?" came the reply. (If he knew what was coming he didn't show it. There was no small talk. No "How are you? Allow me to introduce myself. This is my card. Did you see the game last night?" The lawyer came straight to the point.)

"What have I got to do in order to live for ever?"

"What does the law say? What do you make of it all?" Jesus replied.

(He obviously knew that lawyers like nothing better than to show off their knowledge in front of others.)

The top lawyer cleared his throat in that ladies-and-gentlemen-of-the-jury-you'd-better-listen-to-this-because-you-need-someone-of-my-intelligence-to-put-you-straight way that lawyers do. "Love God with everything you've got and love your neighbour in the way you love yourself." (Which may well have been hard in his case, because you get the impression he loved himself a lot.)

"That's right," answered Jesus. "If you do that you certainly will live for ever."

Thank you, the lawyer thinks to himself. At least Jesus recognises the genius before him. "But I have a further question, if you don't mind. You see... Well... Who exactly is my neighbour?"

"It's like this," came the reply...

The way to Jericho is down,
And if you leave from J'rusalem town,
Try not to meet a thief or a robber
Who'll bash you up and steal your clobber.

For so it happened to a chap
Who walked feet first into a trap.
A group of thugs gave him what for
And left his body on the floor.

His clothes all gone, his money nicked,
His bleeding face all bruised and kicked,
Unless someone came round the bend
He knew his life was at an end.

It wasn't long before a priest
On broken bones his eyes did feast.
He looked away, his face to hide
And walked by on the other side.

A Levite came upon the spot –
By now the blood had formed a clot.
He heard a moan and then a cry,
So said a prayer and scurried by.

A Samaritan then came along
Whistling a happy, catchy song,
He stopped when he glanced down to see
The poor bloke writhe in agony.

As quick as quick he patched him up
And gave him wine – though not to sup –
To rub with oil into his head
(It helps when you've been left half-dead.)

"You need some rest and lots of grub,
I'll take you to the local pub."
He plonked him on his donkey's back
And off they set along the track.

The place he knew was warm and bright —
The ideal spot to spend the night.
The sort of inn where, when you wake,
You've soon forgot that dreadful ache.

"Here, take these coins, my landlord friend,
Buy stuff to help his body mend.
Should it cost more, then you just say,
I'll pay next time I'm down this way."

"Which of those three was good and kind?"
"The one who helped, I think you'll find."
"Quite right," said Jesus — it was he
Who'd told the tale so cleverly.

"I know what your type's all about.
You've tried and failed to catch me out.
Now stop this silly question game.
If you love God, go do the same!"

FACTS

THE SAMARITANS ONLY CONSIDERED THE FIRST FIVE BOOKS OF THE OLD TESTAMENT TO BE IMPORTANT, WHEREAS THE JEWS USED THE WHOLE OF THE OLD TESTAMENT.

Now, the problem with this story is that the title in most Bibles is wrong. You see, to those people listening to Jesus there never was and never could be such a thing as a *good* Samaritan. Everybody knew they were bad. Just like today everyone knows that _____ are bad. (Fill in as you wish. My editor advises me that if *I* do it, I could get sued.) The Samaritans and the Jews (Jesus' people who lived in Israel) were great enemies and rivals, like Everton and Liverpool, Man Utd and Man City and so on. The last person in the world a Jew would call "good" was a Samaritan or the other way round for that matter.

SAMARITANS LIVED IN SAMARIA. HERE'S ONE OF THE
WORST JOKES EVER ABOUT THE BIBLE:
WHO'S THE FATTEST PERSON IN THE BIBLE?
THE WOMAN OF SAMARIA! (GROAN!)

We only give the story the title "The good Samaritan" because we know how it ended. Jesus deliberately makes the Samaritan the hero. Not the Jewish priest or the Levite. (No, he didn't wear particular jeans, he was another type of religious person.)

TONGUE
TWISTER!

LEE VOIGHT, THE LEVITE WORE
TIGHT LEVI JEANS

So, as he listened to the story the lawyer may have begun to sweat because a bad person is helping out. In a very clever way, Jesus was challenging him about everything he'd ever thought. When Jesus finished the story, he asked him which man was the neighbour to the one who needed help. There was only one answer, but the lawyer couldn't even bear to say the word "Samaritan". He mumbled something about the kind person being the neighbour.

To finish off, Jesus said, "Well, in that case, you go and do the same." Or to put it another way: even the people you hate are your neighbours. Show them love. That's the sort of love that will get you to live for ever!

GO+Cha!

Luke 10:25–37

Be happy!

The Pharisees loved to moan and complain and find fault with everyone and everything. They were never happier than when they were miserable.

And Jesus made them miserable. Or rather, what he was doing made them miserable. For instance, they didn't like the fact that he mixed with bad people. (Some of these bad people were tax collectors. Your parents may think they're bad people today, but as the son of a father who used to be one, I have to disagree.) Back then nobody liked tax collectors because they worked for the dreaded Romans. It was reckoned they creamed off some of the tax for themselves.

The Pharisees were so against Jesus mixing with people like this that they weren't able to see the good effect Jesus was having on them. (Elsewhere, Jesus explains the reason that he's with bad people is to help them be good – after all, nobody complains to doctors because they spend time with people who are unwell.)

RECEPTIONIST AT A DOCTOR'S SURGERY ON THE PHONE:

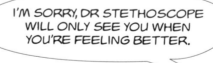

I'M SORRY, DR STETHOSCOPE WILL ONLY SEE YOU WHEN YOU'RE FEELING BETTER.

So Jesus decided to tell some parables to catch them out.

Counting sheep

Just imagine we've got a flock of 100 sheep. Each day ewe count them all to check they're all OK. Then, one day to ewer horror, ewe discover that one of them is missing. Thanks to the government's

numeracy programme, ewe are able to work out that ewe've now only got 99 sheep. So what do ewe do? Ewe leave those unlost 99 sheep and go off searching for the stray. Then as soon as ewe've found it, ewe scoop it onto ewer shoulders and dash back to tell ewer friends.

"Look everyone. I've found the lost sheep. Be happy with me!"

Of course everyone is going to be happy for you. They'll be as pleased as you are.

Well, if that's what happens when a human is happy over finding a lost sheep, then just imagine how happy everybody in heaven will be when a lost person is found. And what Jesus meant by that was that he was finding people who were lost, people who didn't know about God or what he wanted. He was picking them up and taking them back to safety.

And it was brilliant. In fact, finding one lost sheep was better than having 99 sheep that never got lost in the first place.

You'd have thought that after being lambasted in this way, the Pharisees and legal experts would be feeling a bit sheepish. But they weren't. Because Jesus knew their thinking was still a bit woolly, he rammed another story their way.

It's the same idea but you just substitute coins for sheep.

I coin't find it

A woman has ten coins. Nice and bright and shiny. Worth nearly £1,000 in today's money. Then she loses one of them at home... £100 gone missing. Oh no! What's she going to do? Something I bet you've never done. She gets the brightest light she can find and sweeps the house as thoroughly as she can. She checks every speck of dust, moves all the cushions, shifts all the furniture... until there it is. Lurking down the back of the sofa – her precious coin.

She's so pleased that she rushes out (hopefully after having put the coin safely with the other nine) and tells all her friends and neighbours that she's found it.

"Be happy with me. I've found that coin I thought I'd lost."

You note, of course, that Jesus didn't tell this story about a man. It is a well-known fact that most objects lost in a home are discovered by women – usually patient, kind mothers/grans and so on.)

"That's how excited the angels get when just one bad person stops being bad and does what God wants," said Jesus.

Perhaps the best-known story Jesus told on this idea is one that we call the Prodigal Son, which is a shame really. Why? Because no one ever uses the word "prodigal", let alone has a clue what it means. Or do they? See if you can prove me wrong.

Which of these sentences do you think shows its true meaning?

(a) The long jumper made a prodigal leap of over 8 metres.

(b) The boy was poked and prodigalled by the bullies in his class.

(c) The boy's spending on sweets had been rather prodigal and now he felt sick.

(d) Whilst on holiday, the family stayed in the quiet village of Prodigal.

The answer is (c). It means being wasteful and throwing your money about. So it would be better to call this story the Wasteful Son. But even then it doesn't do the story justice. Remember – what Jesus is talking about is people who aren't happy when someone turns back to God.

Why don't you read the story and make up a title that fits better?

Dodgy lad returns to dad

There was a man whose younger son
Decided that he wanted fun.
"I'd like the cash," to Dad he said,
"That I should get when you are dead."

So Father split his money up
And gave half to the cheeky pup,
Who, once he did the swag receive,
Shot off without a "By your leave".

He headed for a distant land
Where money flowed from out his hand.
Before you could say, "Steady on!"
The jolly lot was spent and gone.

PARABULZ

Though life seemed bad with empty purse
It soon all went from bad to worse.
Food prices soared when famine struck.
Friends left him to his rotten luck.

By now his tum began to throb,
So off he went to find a job.
A farmer said, "Go feed my swine,"
And so he helped those piggies dine.

And while he watched pork bellies fill,
He wished that he could scoff their swill.
"One taste," he said, "would be all right!"
But no one gave a single bite.

One day he woke from his nightmare.
"My father's men have food to spare,
And here I am, thin as a rake.
I've really made a big mistake."

"I'll go to Dad, confess my sin.
Perhaps he'll even let me in,
And if I find he's not too gruff
Life as his slave won't be that rough."

But when the father saw his face,
He scurried at a cracking pace
To cuddle him, while tears of joy
Flowed from his eyes onto the boy.

Who, full of shame, tried to explain
Why he was coming home again.
But his old man, he didn't care.
What mattered was his son was there!

"Quick, servants, there's no time to lose.
Go get my boy robe, ring and shoes.
Pinch me, do! – it can't be real
And if it is, let's cook some veal!"

"I thought the boy was dead, you see,
But now he's come back home to me.
Once lost, he's found outside my gate.
Let's have some nosh and celebrate.

"Call caterers to do their stuff.
Only the best is good enough."
Then neighbours were invited in
To eat and drink and make much din.

But then the elder of the boys,
Returning, heard the joyful noise.
"What's happening?" he asked a lad.
"Your brother's back – I bet you're glad."

"Big deal," said he and turned to go,
"I'll not go in with him, you know."
His dad appeared. "Come in," he said,
But now this son was seeing red.

"I've every right to rant and rave,
For years I've stayed here as your slave.
I've ploughed your field, I've kept your herd
And listened to your every word.

"For me you couldn't spare a quid
To buy my friends a tasty kid.
When Waster comes you smile and laugh.
He even gets a fatted calf!"

"My son, calm down. Enter these doors.
What's left one day will all be yours.
Tonight, please, let good cheer abound,
Your brother who was lost is found!"

FACTS

JEWS THOUGHT OF PIGS AS UNCLEAN ANIMALS AND
WOULDN'T GO NEAR THEM, LET ALONE EAT PORK
CHOPS, BACON OR HAM.

PARABULZ

So what do you think? Thought of a better title?

At the end of the day it doesn't really matter. What does matter is that we all get the point. Jesus was doing a Gotcha on the Pharisees. He was showing them very clearly that instead of telling him off for trying to help lost people, they should be pleased when just one of them turned from being bad and chose to follow God.

These stories can all be found in Luke 15. (The sheep one also appears in Matthew 18:10–14.) Don't forget to read the first two verses of the chapter to understand the reason why Jesus told them.

Jesus wasn't the only person to tell Gotcha stories, but this chapter is long enough already. You'll have to go to Chapter 6 of this book if you want to find the other ones.

5. What are you like?

Like most people, Jesus enjoyed going out for meals. At least it would seem as though he did, because we often read about him eating out or visiting an old friend.

FACTS

THE JEWS ATE A LOT OF FOOD THAT WE RECOGNISE. THEY ALSO HAD OTHER FOODS WE DON'T EAT MUCH, SUCH AS MEDLAR, CAROB AND MY FAVOURITE, SPELT (SPELT "S P E L T"). JUST IN CASE YOU'RE WONDERING, SPELT IS A TYPE OF GRAIN. ITALIANS CALL IT *FARRO* AND GERMANS, FOR REASONS BEST KNOWN TO THEMSELVES, CALL IT *DINKLE*.

Menu

Spellt cheese sandwich

Soup with large sppelt roll

LOOK, THEY'VE MISSPELT SPELT!

A story in a story

One day Jesus had been invited round to the house of Simon, a Pharisee. While lying at the table, (they didn't sit like we do, but lay

down alongside a low table, leaning on their left arm), an unknown woman sneaked into the house. She clearly wanted to see Jesus. She crept up, her face wet with tears. Not only that, but as she got close to him her tears splashed onto his feet. As soon as she realised that she was getting his feet wet, she fell down on her knees and tried to wipe them dry with the only thing she had to hand – her hair. Covering his feet with kisses, she then poured a jar of expensive perfume over them.

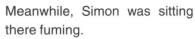

TODAY, PEOPLE USE THE WORD 'PHARISEE' TO MEAN SOMEONE WHO PAYS ATTENTION TO THE SMALLEST OF RULES AND SO THINKS THEY ARE BETTER THAN PEOPLE WHO AREN'T BOTHERED BY REGULATIONS.

Meanwhile, Simon was sitting there fuming.

"If this Jesus were so special he'd realise what a bad person this woman is. He certainly wouldn't allow her to carry on in the way that she is."

But he didn't say anything out loud, presumably for the same reason your mum or dad tell you not to make comments about people who come round to your house for a meal – even when you desperately want to.

But it looked as though Jesus knew what he was thinking. "Simon," he said, "I've got a little story for you… There were once two men. They both owed some money to another person. One of them owed roughly £40,000 and the other owed about £4,000. But sadly for both of them, neither had any money to pay the other person back. But it didn't matter, because the man who had lent the money in the first place called them together and told them that he would let them off the amount they owed him."

(Warning: Do not try borrowing this sort of money at home. Your mum or dad or gran or whoever won't be too pleased. In fact, it's best not to try it anywhere. If you want my advice, it's best not to owe anybody anything if you can possibly help it.)

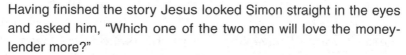

MUM, ABOUT THAT £40,000 I OWE YOU...

Having finished the story Jesus looked Simon straight in the eyes and asked him, "Which one of the two men will love the money-lender more?"

"Well, I suppose it's going to be the one who owed the most money in the first place. He'll be more pleased about being let off the hook."

"You're right of course," answered Jesus.

There was a slight pause, as Jesus shifted round to look at the woman.

"Look Simon. Can you see that woman?" (An obvious question. Jesus knew the answer!) "I've come into your house at your invitation. You haven't given me anything so I can wash my dirty feet."

(In a hot, dusty land the host provided guests with water to clean their feet.)

"But this woman has washed my feet with her tears. You haven't welcomed me with a kiss. But this lady has hardly stopped kissing my feet as soon as she got here."

(And I think even kissing the feet of Jesus can't have been the most pleasant experience in the world.)

"You haven't given me any refreshing perfume for my head and hair. But this woman whom you dislike has poured out her whole jar on my feet."

PARABULZ

Action	Simon	Woman
Food	√	x
Wash Feet	x	√
Kiss	x	√
Perfume	x	√
Jesus impressed	x	√

Here comes the clever bit. If I were to ask you who loved Jesus more in this story, the woman or Simon, you'd have to say the woman. Pretty obvious, isn't it? She's been doing all the things Simon ought to have done. And the reason she loves Jesus so much is that she's been let off a great amount. Not of money. That isn't mentioned. But of *sin*. She's been let off from a big pile of sin – in other words, she's been forgiven for all the bad stuff she's ever done. And, says Jesus, this is what happens when someone realises they have been let off big time – they love big time in return. On the other hand, if a person has only been let off a little bit, they only love a little back.

To make the point absolutely clear, Jesus turned to the woman and explained that her sins have been forgiven. Just so she was sure. You see, Simon was half right. He knew what a very bad person the woman was. He was cross because Jesus didn't seem to realise this. But Jesus did. He knew the woman was sorry for being bad – and he just let her show how grateful she was by letting her do all those kind things for him.

Luke 7:36–50

Perfect your praying

Jesus' disciples wanted him to teach them how to pray. So he told them a story about a grumpy person. What has a grumpy person got to do with praying, I hear you ask?

You've got a friend. In fact, you've got two friends. One of them comes to you very late at night. At midnight. So you decide to have a midnight feast, seeing as it's midnight (which, as everyone knows, is the best time for midnight feasts).

But you haven't got any food. So you go to your other friend.

"Friend," you say, "another friend of mine has turned up on my doorstep. I'd like to give him something to eat. But I haven't got anything to eat. What are the chances...?"

"Go away," says the not-so-friendly friend. "The door's locked. We're all tucked up in bed. I can't help you, I'm afraid. Goodnight."

"But you're my friend!" you shout.

"Not tonight I'm not. Go home!"

But you don't. Instead you keep hammering away on the door until the friend (the one in bed, not the one who's waiting to be fed at your house) flings off his bedcovers, storms downstairs, goes to the cupboard, finds some bread, unlocks the door and shoves the food into your outstretched arms.

"You're a great friend," you say to him.

"Bah," he replies. "I'm not doing this to be friendly. I'm doing this to make you go away so I can get some sleep!"

He slams the door. You go home and have your midnight feast – well, it's a bit after midnight now, but it doesn't really matter because you've got what you wanted.

So how does that help us with praying?

You can find the answer in Luke 11:5–13. If you're like the grumpy person and can't be bothered, I'll explain it for you. But only on the condition that you don't have a midnight feast within the next week. The point that Jesus goes on to explain is this:

1   It's good to keep on asking God for something, even if your prayers don't seem to be answered straight away.

2   God, who is the one listening to our prayers, is far kinder than that grumpy person. In fact, he's even kinder than the kindest of dads. God, who's never bad, will always give us exactly the best thing for us.

So whatever you do, keep on praying!

Rich but stupid

When we're really young, we tend to squabble with our brothers and sisters about who can watch which programme on the telly (me), who should have the last scoop of ice cream (me) or who's turn it is to tidy up the room (you).

When we get older we can still argue about these things, but we add other situations too. Like who gets money when a relative dies. And sometimes everyone gets so cross that they drag lawyers in to sort it out, so everyone gets less money... except the lawyers who have to be paid.

Instead of getting a lawyer, one man asked Jesus to sort out his problem.

"Tell my brother to share the money with me!" he asked. (No, "please", "would you mind?", or even trying to explain the situation. Just an order.)

Jesus told him that it wasn't his job to sort out this sort of situation. Then he went on to say...

A rich man had some land. It was very good, fertile land and in due course produced a fantastic amount of crops. In fact, to be honest, there were too many. He had nowhere to put it all. All the barns he owned put together weren't large enough to store it all and he had to be careful that it wasn't going to go to waste. Suddenly he came up with this idea.

"I know what I'll do. I'll knock down the small barns I've got at the moment and then I'll build some bigger ones. So big that I can put not only these fantastic crops in them, but all my possessions. That ought to set me up for the rest of my life. I can take things easy and have a good time without a care in the world."

But there was just one problem. He didn't know that at the same time he was thinking all this, God was thinking too. But he found out about it pretty soon, because God spoke to him.

YOU FOOL! YOU'RE GOING TO DIE THIS VERY NIGHT. WHO'S GOING TO GET ALL YOUR CROPS, BELONGINGS AND PLANS THEN?

What point do you think Jesus is trying to make in this story?

(a) Watch out for greed, in any shape or form.

(b) There's more to life than how much you've got.

(c) If you just look out for yourself without thinking about God, all your plans will come to nothing in the end.

It's all three. Of course, it doesn't mean that if you've got a lot of money you're going to die just as you are about to enjoy yourself. This is a warning to use your money wisely on the sort of things that God values – not just spending it on yourself. It's also a reminder that we can all make plans about what's going to happen in the future, but only God knows what will take place. It's best not to pin our hopes too much on tomorrow without doing the right thing today.

Luke 12:13–21

I was sitting there!

Do you have a special seat at meal times? Or, at a birthday party, do you try to get next to the person whose birthday it is, just to show that you are a special friend? Jesus was at a house where that happened.

Jesus noticed that everyone was choosing the best seats. Perhaps they were arguing about who should sit where, or maybe they got in early just to make sure of their place. They might even have put down their coat, to stake a claim.

"Imagine you are at a wedding," Jesus began. "Whatever you do, don't plonk yourself down in one of the special places. The chances are that someone far more important will have been invited. You'll be really embarrassed if the person who sent out the invitations brings this other person to where you are sitting and says, 'Excuse me, this seat is for my distinguished friend here.' You'll have to move to sit in the worst spot of all. What's more, everybody will be watching you and shaking their heads, thinking, 'Serves them right, the poser.'

"Instead, what you should do is go and find the least important place and sit yourself down there. If you do that, the host will come up and say, 'You can't possibly sit there. I've a much better seat for you. Come with me.' Then he'll march you up to the front, in full view of the other guests, who'll whisper to each other, 'I don't know who that person is, but they're obviously somebody special.'"

"That's the way it is," Jesus finished. "Everybody who thinks they're better than they are has a big shock coming to them. But the modest people will be the ones to get recognised in the end."

Or to put it another way:

GBISDEAH TGE TSHAW CINGOM OT HETM TUB HET BEHULM
LILW EB EDAM A SUFS FO

Luke 14:7-11

The cunning man with the cunning plan

FACTS

*A BUSHEL = 2 BUCKETS. A BUCKET = 2 PECKS. A PECK = 8 QUARTS. A QUART = 2 PINTS. TWO PECKS IN A BUCKET… WEIRD. FOR THOSE OF YOU WHO PREFER THE METRIC SYSTEM A BUSHEL IS 35.239 LITRES, WHICH IS EASIER TO COPE WITH BUT LESS FUN.

Now, if you're anything like me, you're probably thinking, What's going on here? Is Jesus saying that it's good to be sneaky and dishonest and swindle your boss out of money, to your own advantage? I thought he would have been against that sort of thing.

But before we all get uptight trying to work out what's going on, we have to listen to what Jesus said after he'd told this story.

He said that people who don't follow him are often better at coping in the harsh world where everyone is out for himself. Very often they will be cleverer and wiser in the way they deal with situations – like the manager who was about to be fired. He used his position and money to win friends so that when the hard times came, there would be plenty of people he could rely upon.

Jesus told his followers to use their money to win friends, so that when they ran out of it, they would get a warm welcome, not in people's houses but in God's kingdom.

 Makes you think, doesn't it? And that, as I said at the beginning of the book, is one of the things that Jesus liked to do. Make people think. Apart from buying ten copies of this book to give to friends, how do you think you could use your money? Are you a cunning person with a cunning plan?

Luke 16:1–13

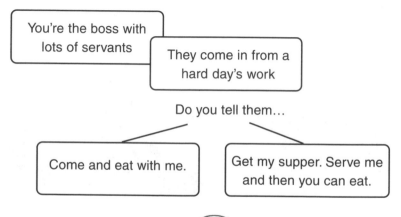

You're dutiful. It's true

You're the boss with lots of servants

They come in from a hard day's work

Do you tell them…

Come and eat with me.

Get my supper. Serve me and then you can eat.

If you're the boss, then you tell them to cook you your meal. If you're the servant, how should you feel?

You should simply say, "I was only doing what I was supposed to do." It rather reminds me of a story of my own.

I used to live in Italy with my wife and family. One summer, my wife's parents came to visit us. My father-in-law went out for a walk one day and discovered some money just lying in the road. He brought it back to our house. We counted it up and there were hundreds of thousands. Before you get too excited, I must say that in those days Italians used lira, not euros, and there were about 2,000 lira to one British pound. It was still a lot of money – probably several hundred pounds.

So we went to the local shop and told the lady there that we'd found some cash and if anyone had lost any, they should come to us. Sure enough, later that day a rather upset woman came along saying that she'd lost some money. When we asked her how much, she told us exactly the same amount that my wife's father had found. It was the money she had saved to pay for her rent and she was worried that she wouldn't be able to pay now. It was clearly hers, so we gave it to her.

Well, even later that day she returned with a huge ice cream cake to say "Thank you". We tried to tell her that she needn't have bothered, after all the money was hers all along and we were only doing what was right. But she insisted that we take it. So, being

very sensible, we ate it all up – after all, if there's one thing that Italians know how to do, it's ice cream. Oh and pasta, sunshine, beautiful buildings, beaches, friendliness, football – well, you get the idea.

The point of the story is this. We felt we shouldn't be rewarded just for doing the right thing. We thought that if the world got to the point where people only helped others or did as they were told just to get something out of it, then it wouldn't be a very nice place.

I think that's the point Jesus is making here. When it comes to doing stuff for God, then we should just get on with it as dutiful servants.

By the way, if you think we were mad for owning up to having found the money, you're not the only ones. All our neighbours in Italy thought we were crazy too.

Luke 17:7–10

Mr Big and Mr No Name

If there's one type of person who's guaranteed to get up everybody's nose, it is the girl or boy who think and acts as if they are so much better than everyone else.

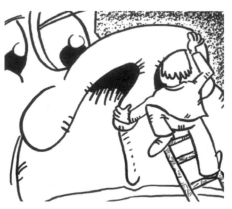

They may think they're better at playing the flute, kicking a football or speaking French. It doesn't matter. Sometimes you just want to blow them out of your nose, wrap them up with the other stuff that's up there, and throw them in a waste paper basket. Jesus didn't go that far, but he certainly told a parable to get people to stop being so obnoxious. I wonder if you know who the people in question were?

Yes, you've guessed. It was the Pharisees.

It was time to go to the synagogue, the place where the Jews worshipped God. Mr Big stepped out of his house, and his long, flowing, richly coloured robe flipped out too. It was the best, most expensive robe that money could buy. He was cool and he liked everyone to know it. As he swept along the street, everyone turned their heads and the children dodged out of his way. What a sight he was. Cool, a great dresser and what's more, a Pharisee, someone who knew the most about God.

At the same time another man, Mr No Name, left home. He was one of those people you wouldn't like to meet down a dark alley, smelly, shifty looking and clearly up to no good. People got out of his way too, but for different reasons. He was a tax collector, a swindler and a nasty bit of work.

The two men's paths were taking them to the synagogue (the place where Jewish people worship) and they arrived at the same time. Mr Big made a dramatic entrance, coughing loudly so that people would know he was there. Quietly and sneakily, Mr No Name slipped into the building but hung around at the back in the shadows where he hoped no one would spot him.

With a quick look round to make sure every eye was on him, Mr Big suddenly pulled himself up to his full height and began to pray. His voice boomed out and the sound of it echoed around the roof.

"Ahem. God! Thank you so much that I'm not like so many bad people, thieves, the wicked or those who cheat on their wives. And I certainly thank you that I'm not like that revolting tax collector lurking in the darkness over there."

He pointed vaguely in the direction of Mr No Name, who shrunk back into the corner as everyone turned to look, stare and shake their heads. Mr Big paused.

"Anyway, as I was saying, God, I'm not like them at all. In fact I go without food two days a week and give away one tenth of all my income. So thank you once again for making me such a splendid person."

It was a good prayer. One or two of those who heard it wanted to cheer.

Mr No Name slumped to his knees. His eyes were fixed on the dust beneath his feet. "I'm sorry, God. Please forgive me for being such a bad man."

If we'd been there at the time, listening to Jesus telling this story, we'd probably have agreed with the Pharisee. After all, he was very fortunate not to have been a bad person, and was so clearly blessed by God. If we had a choice we'd probably rather have been like him. But Jesus didn't think like that. He told those listening that it was the bad man, the tax collector, who pleased God. He was the one with the right attitude. God was pleased with him, not the full-of-it Pharisee.

As Jesus explained, and as we've already discovered, those who are puffed up with pride like some over-inflated balloon will explode in shame and unhappiness. Those who don't think they're anything special will actually be treated as if they were kings.

Luke 18: 9–14

If you do that once more I'll...

There are many annoying things about brothers and sisters. One of them is that they know better than most how to upset us and do things we don't like. I've left a space so you can write down some of the other annoying things about them. I hope there's enough space... although I doubt it.

(But remember, if you write a lot they could probably do the same!)

It can be hard to know how many times we have to let them say sorry, knowing that they'll be back up to their tricks again as soon as they can.

At least I bet that's how Jesus' friend Peter felt.

"How many times should I forgive my brother when he does something wrong? Is seven times about enough? What do you think, Jesus?"

"I don't think seven is enough. What about 77 times? You see, there was..." At this point Peter knew he was in for a parable...

There was once a king wanted to sort out his finances. (That's a lot easier than sorting out his fiancées, but that's another story, and one which Jesus didn't tell.)

This king had all the servants who were in charge of the money brought to him. The first one owed him quite a bit. When I say quite a bit, what I really mean is a lot. Millions and millions in fact. So in comes this servant, knees knocking and teeth chattering.

"You owe me a lot of money," boomed the king. "I want it now!"

But, like you and me, he didn't have it.

So the king said, "Give me your wife and family, then. I'll sell them together with you and see if I can get at least some of the cash you owe me."

At this point the man flung himself down on his knees, begging for mercy.

"Please give me more time. I'll pay back everything I owe you as soon as I can."

The king was a kind sort and his heart went out to the man.

"Don't worry. You won't need to pay back anything. I'll let you off all the debt. You won't have to pay anything."

Well, the man thought his birthday had come early. He left the king, skipping and whistling as he went. Nothing was going to get to him that day... until he came across one of the men he worked with.

It so happened that this particular man owed him a few pounds. The first man snapped, "Where's that money you owe me? Have you got it yet?"

He grabbed hold of the other man's throat and began to strangle him in his anger.

The second man dropped on his knees and began to cry, "N... n... n... no, I haven't. If you just give me a little bit more time, I'll be able to pay you back."

"A likely story," snorted the first man. "I know your sort. You'll keep me waiting forever and always come up with some excuse. A spell in prison will sort you out. Then you'll come up with the money soon enough!"

So he had him thrown into jail, and stormed off fuming with rage. But what he didn't know was that he had been seen by other people. They were pretty upset at the way their friend had been treated. Together they decided to go to the king and tell him what had happened.

As soon as he heard their story, the king ordered the first servant to come and see him immediately.

"What on earth is this I've just heard about you? A while ago you were in here on your hands and knees pleading with me to let you off the huge debt you owed. And I took pity on you and cancelled the lot. Now I hear how you've treated your colleague."

The king was pretty steamed up by now.

"You should have learnt from me and shown some kindness towards him. Because of what you've done, I've changed my mind."

He turned to the captain of the royal guard. "Take this man to prison and keep him there until he pays every last penny that he owes me."

Jesus makes it pretty clear that if God has forgiven you and yet you can't find it in yourself to forgive someone else, then he's not going to think much of the way you behave.

Matthew 18:21–35

6. OT Gotchas

Long before Jesus started doing Gotchas, there were a few knocking around in the Old Testament (which is the bit of the Bible that tells what happened before Jesus was born).

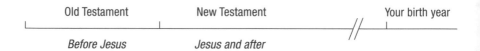

Those of you sensible enough to read *10 Rulz* will have read about David, one of the greatest kings Israel ever had.

FACTS

DAVID AND HIS DESCENDANTS RULED FOR OVER 400 YEARS — A LONG TIME! FOR MOST OF THAT TIME HE LIVED IN JERUSALEM. SEE THE MAP ON PAGE 71.

Sadly, he didn't always do the right thing. In one period of his life, he managed to break three of God's 10 Rulz in a very short space of time.

1 He wanted to have someone else's wife for himself.
2 He slept with this wife, which the Bible calls adultery.
3 He arranged for her husband to be murdered.

David's school report	
Harp playing	Shows great promise (well done)
Stealing	Good at this (sadly)
Adultery	Shows promise (sadly)
Murder	Done this (sadly)
Overarm throwing	Practises hard and getting better (well done)

So God arranged for David to get a Gotcha. He sent a wise man called Nathan to speak to the king.

Katching the king (Part 1)

Nathan: Hail, King David!

David: What? Hail? But it hasn't even been snowing! What are you talking about, man?

Nathan: I don't mean that sort of hail. I mean, "hello" hail.

FACTS

GOD ONCE SENT HAIL ONTO EGYPT AS A WAY OF PUNISHING THE PHARAOH WHO WOULDN'T LET THE ISRAELITES LEAVE HIS COUNTRY.

David: Oh, I see. Very well. Why have you come to see me today?

Nathan: I'm going to tell you a story.

David: Oh, great. I love stories. And if I like it enough I might even make it into a psalm and we can sing it at the temple. Anyway, get on with it, man. We haven't got all day. Talking of which, do you want to hear my latest? It's all about sheep and God and still waters. I'm going to call it 23!

Nathan: Two men lived in the same town. One was stinking rich and the other was dirt poor.

David: Stinking Rich and Dirk Poor? What funny names!

Nathan: Those weren't their names. That's what they were. One of them was stinking rich – he had lots of money. The other was dirt poor –

he didn't. Anyway as I was saying, the rich man – let's call him Rich – was absolutely loaded. He had sheep and cows coming out of his eyeballs.

David: Yuk. That must have been painful.

Nathan: *(to himself)* They're not the only things that are painful around here... *(loudly)* The other man, we'll call him Dirk, had nothing, except one ewe.

David: He had a me? Oh good. Am I in this story too?

Nathan: A ewe. Not a you. It's a female sheep.

David: I know, I know. I used to be a shepherd. Remember?

Nathan: As I was saying, all Dirk had was a ewe. He had seen it born and cared for it ever since then – letting it eat and drink with the rest of the family. Sometimes when he flopped into bed at the end of a busy day it would nuzzle up to him and fall asleep in his arms.

David: Ah, I think I'm going to cry. *(blows his nose loudly in hanky)*

Nathan: One fine summer day Rich had a visitor, so he needed to give him something to eat. Instead of picking one of his own fat sheep he went and took Dirk's sheep. He killed it and served it as lamb for his guest.

(Pause. David springs to his feet.)

David: That's a dreadful story! What a horrible man Rich is. If I ever get my hands on him I'll sort him out. He deserves to be executed. The least he can do is to repay Dirk four times the cost of the lamb. I've never heard of such a mean, uncaring act.

Nathan: Gotcha!

David: What do you mean, "Gotcha"?

Nathan: You are Rich.

David: Well, yes, I know I've got lots of fine things. If a king can't be rich, then who can?

Nathan: No, I mean you are the man Rich. I was telling a story about you. That's what you've done. God has given you the whole kingdom. He took it from the last king, Saul, and gave everything to you. You had at least enough wives for one royal girl band and yet you chose to take another one who was already married to someone else. And then you murdered her husband.

Finally David realised what a mistake he'd made. Sadly, the damage was already done, and his family all suffered as a result of his wickedness. Interestingly enough, he did write a song about it all. You can read it in Psalm 51. Although he had done an awful thing, David knew that God had also forgiven him. He wrote this song to tell the world about it. It's a fantastic psalm and reading it is a very good way of admitting things to God when we've done things he doesn't like.

TOP OF THE POPS
1 "I have sinned" – (King David, Ballad No. 51)
2 "Singing in the hail" – (King David, Chorus No. 231)
3 "Shepherd's songs" – (King David, Ballad No. 23)

2 Samuel 12:1–12

Even though God had forgiven David, he told him that his family was going to go through some very bad experiences. Sure enough, that's what happened. Two of his sons quarrelled and one called Absalom killed his brother, Amnon. When he'd done that, Absalom ran away and stayed clear of his father for over three years. David wanted to see him again, but he didn't seem to do anything about it. One of David's close friends, Joab, knew that David needed a push to make him order his son back from exile so he sent a woman to speak to the king. He told her exactly what to say and even how to dress up.

Katching the king (Part 2)

Now before you read on, what do you think Joab told her to say? Remember – this is a book about parables, a chapter about Gotchas, and the aim is to make David realise that he's doing the wrong thing.

Now you've had a chance to think, let's find out.

Woman: Hail, sire!

David: You'll not catch me out on that one. The sun's shining. Look.

Woman: With all due respect, I did warn Your Majesty.

David: Ooh, that hurt.

Woman: Please help me, O king!

David: O king? Just call me "king". That will be fine. Now, dear lady, tell me why you're looking so miserable.

Woman: My husband is dead, and I'm a widow.

David: Your husband is dead *and* you're a widow. That's awful.

Woman: Yes, well, as I was... er... saying. I have two boys. Good, kind boys they are... or were. You see, they got into a fight and one of them killed the other. As if that wasn't bad enough, all my relatives want me to hand over my surviving son, so they can punish him to death. It's not that they want justice. They know that if I don't have a son and heir, they'll get all my things when I die. That's all they're interested in. If you were to make a royal decree saying that no one was allowed to lay a finger on my son, it would be a great help.

David: I see. Very well, then. I promise that no one will dare touch him.

Woman: Gotcha!

Now this Gotcha is a bit tricky to understand. Basically the point is that the woman tricked David into promising that her son would come to no harm. (Normally, of course, he would have to be executed for the murder of his brother.) So, then she turns the tables on David by saying that his promise ought to cover his son Absalom as well. He shouldn't be put to death for having killed his brother, Amnon.

David realises that he's been caught out and he calls in Joab, telling him to return his son from exile.

2 Samuel 14:1-22

As you've read about King David who got Gotcha'd, you might be tempted to think it has nothing to do with you.

Think again! The worst thing you can do is think that you have nothing to learn from any part of the Bible. David made the mistake of not doing what God had told him to do in the first place, so God sent someone to catch him out. It's always a bad idea to go against anything that God has said. King David never really recovered from what he had done.

We shouldn't be too quick to make judgements. David was caught out because he found it easy to get cross with someone else, while forgetting his own failures.

As Jesus once said... planks, eyes, sawdust and brothers.

(See the beginning of Matthew 7 if you haven't got a clue what I'm talking about. If you haven't had a clue what I've been talking about in any of this book, you could always try giving it away as a present.)

Home Parable Kit

CONTENTS
One Plank
One eye (belonging to a brother)
One speck of sawdust

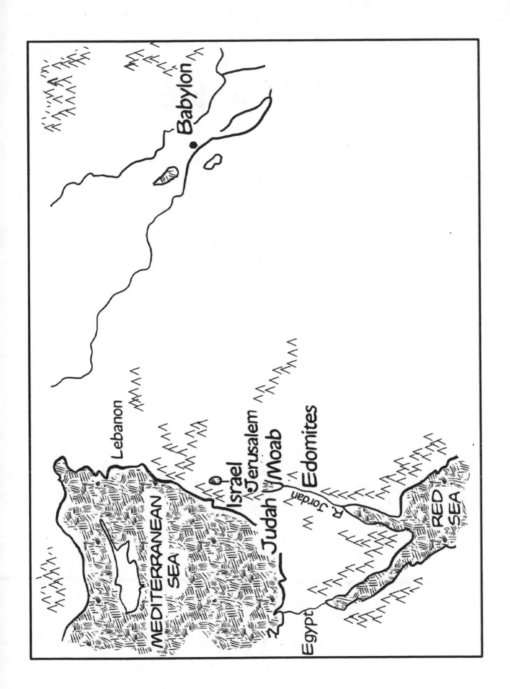

7. OT parabulz

King David wasn't the only king in the Old Testament who had to listen to parables. Amaziah was another king who was on the receiving end of one. See if you can understand what it's all about.

This'll be interesting

RECIPE FOR PLANT PARABLE
INGREDIENTS:
ONE THISTLE (TO BE CRUSHED)
ONE CEDAR TREE
ONE WILD ANIMAL

WHAT YOU DO:

1 TAKE THE THISTLE AND ASK IT TO SEND A MESSAGE TO THE CEDAR TREE.
THE MESSAGE IS TO BE AS FOLLOWS:

My son, Master Thistle, would like to marry your daughter, Miss Cedar. Can you hand her over?

2 AT SOME STAGE, AFTER THE CEDAR HAS GOT THE MESSAGE, ADD A WILD ANIMAL AND MAKE IT TRAMPLE ALL OVER THE THISTLE.

Well, what's all that about then? Good question.

What had happened was that King Amaziah of Judah (aka the Thistle) wanted to fight King Jehoash of Israel. King Jehoash (aka the Cedar) didn't want to fight, so he told Amaziah the parable. The point he was trying to make was that if they had a battle he, King Jehoash, would win and it would all end in tears – just as if a wild animal trod on Amaziah without thinking and possibly even without knowing. But did Amaziah listen? Of course not. He was feeling pretty confident because he'd already duffed up the Edomites, a neighbouring enemy. Sooner or later the kings met at a place called Beth Shemesh. Sadly for Amaziah, it was a complete walkover. His army didn't stand a chance. He was captured and then Jehoash marched on to Jerusalem, pinched a load of stuff out of the temple and then went back home.

Interestingly enough, Amaziah wasn't killed and actually outlived his opponent by 15 years. Bet you'd never have worked all that out from a thistle, a cedar tree and a wild animal!

PARABULZ

Question: And the point is?

Answer: King Amaziah shouldn't have thought that just because he'd beaten the Edomites he would easily beat the Israelites.

Pssst: The map on page 71 will show you where all these places are.

> 2 Kings 14:1-22

Parables are an interesting way to challenge someone to see things differently!

Sometimes parables in the Old Testament part of the Bible were told against places. It wasn't that the place had done anything wrong. It was the people living there that had been bad.

The man who seems to have told the most parables against places was called Ezekiel.

His first target was the city of Jerusalem. He got the idea for the parable straight from God himself.

From babe to babe

One day a man was out walking when he came across a little baby. Years later, when the baby was grown up, this is what he said.

"You'd just been thrown out, unwashed and uncared for. There was no one to take any interest in you. You looked a right mess. So I brought you back from the edge of death. I looked after you and cared for you. Slowly you grew from a dirty, messy baby into a beautiful young woman. You were very attractive – ready to be loved and cared for by someone. In fact, I realised how much I loved you and I took you to be my wife. I spared no expense upon you. You name it, you had it. Jewellery, perfume, expensive clothes, shoes and even a crown on your head as my queen! You ate only the best food prepared by the best cooks ever. Eventually you became so famous that even people living in other countries heard about you. But then tragedy struck…

74

From miss to mess

"...You became obsessed by your beauty and the reputation you had. You got fed up with me – the man who had cared for you and loved you still. Instead, you started chasing after other men. You melted down the gold and silver from the jewellery I had given you and turned them into all sorts of idols and began to worship them as if they were gods. You even killed your sons and daughters, sacrificing them to these idols – the very children that we had once cared for together. Not once did you think back to that day when I found you, cleaned you up and began to look after you. Things got so bad that I punished you in front of all those men you thought loved you. There you were, in a right mess once again."

This was God speaking about the city of Jerusalem – the unwanted baby in the story, who grew up to be a lovely young woman. God was trying to show the people of Jerusalem that thanks to him they had come a long way. He'd looked after them and shown them love and all he got in return was – nothing. Actually it was worse than nothing, because they behaved in a way that didn't even admit to all the good and kind things he had done for them.

Ezekiel 16:1–29

Eagle, cedar, vine, eagle

Ezekiel was told by God to tell another parable, this time to the land of Israel.

A huge eagle was soaring high in the sky when it looked down and there, far below it, was the land of Lebanon. It swooped to the ground and silently shot out its talons at the highest branch of a cedar tree, ripping some of it away. Then it climbed back high into the sky and flew to a far-away land – a land full of businessmen and rich merchants.

FACTS

THE AMERICAN BALD EAGLE IS THE NATIONAL SYMBOL OF AMERICA.

At the end of its long journey it landed in a city where it planted some seed from the branch it had seized in a place where the soil was rich in nutrients. Very soon it began to grow and sprouted more and more branches. Strangely enough, although it had been taken from a cedar tree, the plant was actually a vine. And even more strangely, the branches grew towards the eagle, even though the roots remained firm and solid in the place where they had been planted.

Then another eagle appeared and this time the vine seemed to sense its presence. Its roots stretched out to the eagle, and its branches began feeling out towards this second bird. This time, the vine grew even better than it did before. With the other eagle it had just been a low shrub-like plant, but now it seemed to blossom and grow tall and strong.

And then...

Well. There isn't actually an "and then". That's where it finishes. Not very satisfactory, eh? What's it all about?

The thing about this parable is that it is actually telling a story from the history of the people of Israel. It's in code. And the code appears to be this:

Eagle 1: Nebuchadnezzar (a king who, let's face it, with a name like that would probably prefer being called Eagle 1). He lived in a great city called Babylon.

Lebanon: The land of Judah (that's a bit like calling Scotland, Wales – just to confuse)

Cedar: The important people of Judah.

Seed: King Zedekiah.

Soil: City of Jerusalem.

Eagle 2: Egypt.

Eagle eyes: You, for spotting there's no such character in the story!

So of course, you get it now, don't you?

Nebuchadnezzar goes to Judah and drags the top people off to Babylon. He sends one of them, Zedekiah, back to Jerusalem, where he is in charge but pretty powerless – Zedekiah gets fed up with being a puppet of Babylon and tries to get help from the land of Egypt. It's obvious really! The map on page 71 shows where these places are.

Ezekiel goes on to explain that the idea of getting help from Egypt is doomed to failure. In fact, God is pretty cross because Zedekiah is going back on a treaty that he made with Nebuchadnezzar. This was something that shouldn't have been done.

At the end of the parable there is another one in which God says he himself will plant the vine. Only this time it will really be a great plant. Birds and animals from all over the place will come and find shade in its branches.

If you found all that hard to understand, join the club. But just because it's tricky to get your head round it doesn't mean to say that there isn't a good lesson to learn. (If only the same could be said of school!) There are actually two good points in all of this.

1   It was a bad idea for King Zedekiah to go back on a treaty or agreement made with Nebuchadnezzar. God expects his

people to stick at what they sign up to – whether it's with a friend or even an enemy. Once they've said they're going to do something people should see it through. (Of course that means thinking hard before agreeing to do something we might regret later on.)

2   The best way to grow is by letting God take control. Being like that planted vine that he cared for. Vine not give it a try?

Ezekiel 17

A thorny problem

by
Jothan, son of Jerub-Baal

All the trees of the forest gathered together to sort out who ought to be their king.

Who should it be? Which of us should we choose? The biggest? The oldest? The prettiest? In the end they decided that the olive tree ought to be the one in charge.

FACTS

IN ANCIENT GREECE, THE OLIVE TREE WAS SACRED. ANYONE DAMAGING OR UPROOTING ONE COULD BE SENTENCED TO DEATH.

So they approached the olive tree with their request. But he wasn't interested. "I'm awfully flattered and so on, but I couldn't possibly be king. If I were king I'd have to give up my oil distribution and then what would happen? Everyone loves my oil – men and angels – I can't let them down just to be in charge of the forest. No. I'll not be your king."

So the trees had to have another think about it all. They thought they might have more joy with the fig tree.

FACTS

PLINY, A FAMOUS ROMAN WRITER SAID, "FIGS ARE RESTORATIVE, THE BEST FOOD TO BE EATEN BY ANYONE WHO IS BROUGHT LOW BY LONG SICKNESS AND IS GETTING BETTER. FIGS INCREASE THE STRENGTH OF YOUNG PEOPLE, PRESERVE THE ELDERLY IN BETTER HEALTH AND MAKE THEM LOOK YOUNGER WITH FEWER WRINKLES."

But they got the same sort of response.

"No, no. Being a king is not for me. If I became king when would I ever get time to grow my tasty figs? Everyone would start complaining. After all, you know how delicious they are. It would be a terrible waste. Sorry, but I can't help you."

This wasn't very good, the trees thought. We'd better try to choose someone who will take the job on. They decided that the vine would be a good choice.

FACTS

IN ANCIENT ROME YOU COULD SWAP A BOY FOR TWO JARS OF DRIED GRAPES OR RAISINS.

Whether they were right or not we'll never know, because the vine refused them point-blank. "What? And stop producing this subtle rich red wine? No, I can't be king. There is no way I could ever give up my precious grapes that squeeze out such wine that makes men and angels happy. Thank you and goodbye."

The trees were running out of options. Then someone remembered the thorn bush. Why not make him king? They all thought it was better than nothing so they trooped off to ask him the same question they had asked the others.

FACTS

A ROSE BETWEEN TWO THORNS IS A BEAUTIFUL PERSON WITH UNATTRACTIVE OR UNPLEASANT PEOPLE ON EITHER SIDE OF THEM.

"OK. I'll be your king," the bush said, "but you must do one thing. Come over to me and hide under my branches. If you don't want to do that then a fire will come out of me and burn away all the cedar trees in Lebanon!"

It was all going pretty smoothly until that last bit about the fire. Like most of these Old Testament parables, you need to know a bit about what had gone before.

Jothan, the storyteller, was the youngest of Jerub-Baal's sons. (Jerub-Baal is better known as Gideon.) He was a survivor. His brother, Abimelech, had killed off his other brothers (there were 70 of them!) and Jothan was the only one left. Abimelech had done this because he wanted to be the king. Before he murdered them they had all been in charge of a place called Shechem. But Abimelech had asked the people of Shechem if they wanted to have just one king or 70 kings. When they'd said "One", he went and killed all his brothers. Now he was the only king.

Jotham told the parable to warn the people of Shechem that in making this choice of king they had not gone for a good man, but a prickly, thorny unpleasant person. If they wanted him to protect them, they would get hurt. (You try hiding under a thorn bush for fun and see what he meant!) Was Jotham right?

You'll have to read Judges 9 to find out, but my tip is yes. In fact, the people of Shechem ended up disliking Abimelech so much that they tried to get rid of him. And they would wish they'd never tried.

8. Ready for Jesus

Jesus talked quite a bit about the time when he would come back to earth. He used very vivid and dramatic ideas to explain what it would be like. So he talked about lightning, trumpets, vultures, fig trees, fields and all sorts of things, like weddings. It may come as a surprise to find lightning and vultures mentioned in the same breath as weddings!

FACTS

IN BIBLE TIMES, WEDDING CEREMONIES COULD BE UP TO TWO WEEKS LONG. THE CELEBRATIONS WERE HAPPY OCCASIONS MARKED BY MUSIC AND JOKES LIKE THIS ONE:

A LITTLE BOY ASKED HIS FATHER, "DADDY, HOW MUCH DOES IT COST TO GET MARRIED?"
THE FATHER REPLIED, "I DON'T KNOW, SON. I'M STILL PAYING FOR IT."

$$\frac{10}{10} \text{ for } \frac{5}{10} \text{ and } \frac{0}{10} \text{ for } \frac{5}{10}$$

"OK everyone, it's time to go. He should be here any minute now."

All the girls jumped up in excitement. The bridegroom was coming and it was their job to escort him. It was going to be pretty spectacular. Night had already fallen and so they would guide him through the streets with their lamps.

Oh, did I forget to mention? Some of the girls were pretty bright. Maybe not boffs, but they weren't stupid. Then again, some of them, well, were… stupid, that is. How do we know this? They all had lamps. But only the bright ones knew that to make the lamps work they would also need some oil to set fire to and make the flame. The five bright ones had a little jar full of the sticky liquid. But the stupid ones didn't have anything.

So when the cry went up that the bridegroom had arrived, the girls jumped up and set about trimming the wick on their lamps so they were just the right length for the best flame. Soon ten flames were burning. At least for a short while, but then the stupid girls' lamps began to splutter and flicker.

They said to the bright ones, "Our lamps are going out. Can we have some of your oil?"

"No way," they replied. "If we do that, there might not be enough for everyone. Go and buy some of your own."

They had no option but to do what the others said. Off they scuttled to find someone who was selling oil at that time of night.

While they were out, the bridegroom arrived. The bright girls led him along and the wedding festivities began.

Later, when the stupid girls got back, they banged on the door of the place where the reception was being held.

"Let us in!" they shouted.

But the only reply that came back was, "Who are you? I don't even know who you are!"

Matthew 25:1-13

HOW MANY ACTORS DOES IT TAKE TO LIGHT AN OIL-LAMP?
ONLY ONE. THEY DON'T LIKE TO SHARE THE LAMP-LIGHT!

Back in Bible times, they didn't have karaoke nights or talent shows – as far as we know. They did have other talents, though. They were pieces of money. One talent was worth quite a lot – several hundred pounds. So they were not to be sniffed at.

I said they were not to be sniffed at!

What not to do at a wedding

The chances are that you'll never be asked to hold lamps for someone at a wedding, but if you are, you'll know what to do now. If you ever happen to be a groom (that's the man) at a wedding, it's pretty easy. All you have to do is say "Yes" or "I do" at the right point and everyone thinks you've done a good job. However, if you get invited to a wedding there are plenty of things you shouldn't do. Here are some of them:

1   Don't talk about past boy- or girlfriends of the bride or groom.

2   Don't tread on the bride's dress.

3   Don't listen to the football results during the ceremony.

4   When it gets to the question about there being a good reason for the couple not to marry, don't bring up the fact that the groom once pushed your face in the mud. It's not a good enough reason!

5   Don't let the couple get away without covering them in confetti.

6   Don't say, "What's this?" when someone passes you a canapé. (It's a canapé!)

7   Don't pull funny faces in the photographs. OK, it is the most boring part of the whole day, but you'll be in real trouble when the pictures come back from the photographer.

8   Don't fall asleep during the speeches. Just pretend they aren't too long and are funny.

9   Don't try to dance if there's a disco. You'll embarrass yourself and end up on one of those dreadful TV programmes that show video clips of amusing situations.

10 Don't under any circumstances let the bride's mother kiss you. Even if she says how smart or pretty you look and how grown up you are. If you see her puckering up her lips – run and never look back.

The talent show

A businessman was going off on a long journey, so he called his employees together for a meeting.

"I have to go on a long business trip," he told them, "and while I'm gone I'd like you to look after things here."

He went to his safe and took out some talents.

He gave five to one man, two to another and to the last man he gave just one. Then off he went.

The first man thought about what he could do with the money. He went away and began to put it to good use. The second man did the same and was soon seen busying himself about the place. The third man decided he wouldn't risk losing the money, so he sneaked away, dug a hole and buried it in his garden.

Several weeks later when the businessman came back, he called another meeting of his employees. It had obviously been a good trip. He was grinning from ear to ear.

"Well then," he said, "let's see what you've done with the money I gave you."

The first man stepped forward. His boss looked at him.

"Ah, yes. If I remember correctly I gave you five talents. What have you done with them?"

> SIR, I WENT OUT AND INVESTED THEM AND I MANAGED TO EARN ANOTHER FIVE. SO HERE'S YOUR TEN TALENTS.

"Excellent. Well done. You're just the sort of person I want working for me. Even though I only gave you a few talents it's clear to me that you are someone to be trusted. I've got an important job

PARABULZ

and I can see you're just the man to do it."

He gave the man a warm handshake and turned to the next one.

"Now then. What about you? How did you get on?"

SIR, YOU GAVE ME TWO TALENTS AND I'VE ALSO MANAGED TO EARN SOME MORE. HERE THEY ARE. FOUR TALENTS IN TOTAL, THE TWO YOU GAVE ME PLUS ANOTHER TWO.

"This is fantastic. I can see how fortunate I am to have two trustworthy employees. Well, you'll be pleased to know I've got another job and I want you to do it for me."

He shook his hand too and turned to the final man, who, it has to be said, was looking a bit nervous.

"Ah, yes. You're the man I gave one talent to. What have you done with it?"

WELL, IT'S LIKE THIS. I KNEW YOU WERE A HARD MAN TO PLEASE AND I WAS NERVOUS ABOUT LOSING THE MONEY. SO I DECIDED THE BEST THING TO DO WAS TO HIDE IT IN THE GROUND. HERE IT IS. ALL SAFE AND SOUND!

His boss was fuming.

"So I'm a hard man to please, am I? Well, if you thought that, you could have at least *tried* to please me. You should have put the money in the bank and got some interest on it. Then you would have something to show for yourself. You're just a lazy good-for-nothing."

Then he ordered that the one talent be taken away from him and given to the first man. And the "good-for-nothing" was given the sack.

Getting the sack is when you lose your job. The idea is that a workman would be given a sack when he was about to lose his employment, so that he could put all his tools in it.

SACK

Matthew 25:14–30

Watch it!

You are one of the servants in a big house. Your job is to greet visitors and show them where to go. Sometimes they even give you a tip as you carry their bags, or park their car.

When the owner of the house goes away he leaves you all with strict instructions to keep the house in order. He tells you to keep watch for him and have everything ready for him when he gets back. The only trouble is that he doesn't tell you when he is planning to return. So you have to be ready all the time – in the middle of the night, at the crack of dawn or when the sun is at its highest in the sky.

The important thing is not to be caught out.

Mark 13:32–37

Z

What's it all about, then?

Ever had your teacher leave the classroom for a while and tell you all to get on with your work? What do you do? No... tell the truth! What do you *really* do? Although it is a long time ago, my memory tells me that when the teacher said "Get on with your work!", I usually did the very opposite. I could tell you what happened the time when the teacher came back in and smashed a plate on the floor. Were we in trouble or what? But I won't. (Although we were.)

These parables are all about the time when Jesus is going to come back again. The simple message is get ready and stay ready. Don't think we can do what we like and then suddenly start to do whatever we know we ought to be doing. Why not? Because we've no way of knowing when Jesus is going to turn up. So the best thing is to do what he wants us to do all the time.

How many times do I have to tell you?

If you've never heard your mum or dad or whoever looks after you say that to you, then I can only assume you never listen. Sometimes we're not very good at listening or taking notice of what is being said. It's not even something that happens just when we're young. My family says I never listen. But I hope you'll listen to what Jesus had to say.

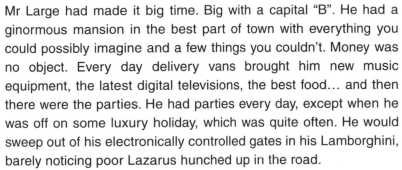

Mr Large had made it big time. Big with a capital "B". He had a ginormous mansion in the best part of town with everything you could possibly imagine and a few things you couldn't. Money was no object. Every day delivery vans brought him new music equipment, the latest digital televisions, the best food… and then there were the parties. He had parties every day, except when he was off on some luxury holiday, which was quite often. He would sweep out of his electronically controlled gates in his Lamborghini, barely noticing poor Lazarus hunched up in the road.

Lazarus was dirty, smelly and he had horrible blotches on his skin because he couldn't afford to go to the doctor to have them checked out. In fact, the only medicine that ever went on these sores was dog saliva. For some reason they loved the taste. When he wasn't lying down, Lazarus would stare through the gates, trying to think what it would be like just to have the chance to eat Mr Large's leftovers. But he never found out.

He died and angels carried him away to heaven.

Strangely, Mr Large also died quite soon afterwards in a helicopter accident while he was doing some off-piste skiing at Aspen in America. There were no angels to carry him to where he was going – a place of misery and suffering…

As he was suffering, Mr Large looked up towards heaven and saw Lazarus standing next to Abraham, a man who had served God all his life. He had nothing to lose so shouted out, "Abraham, sir. Please have pity on me in this dreadful place. Can you send Lazarus down to give me just a sip of water?"

Peering down, Abraham replied, "While you were alive you had everything that you could possibly want. Poor Lazarus here had nothing. Now the tables have been turned and you are the one suffering while he has everything he needs and more. Besides, there's a great gap between where we are and where you are. There's no bridge and no one has ever been able to cross from one side to the other. There's nothing that can be done."

Mr Large thought for a moment. Then he said, "Well, if Lazarus can't come to me is there any chance that you could send him to talk to my brothers? He could warn them not to make the same mistake I've made and end up in this Godforsaken place."

Abraham wasn't convinced. "If it's a warning they need, then all they need to do is open up the Bible and read what Moses and the prophets had to say."

Mr Large took once last chance. "That's all very well and good, but if someone like Lazarus comes to life again they are bound to hear what he has to say and change their lifestyles."

Abraham shook his head. "I'm sorry. If they don't take the trouble to listen to what Moses and the prophets say they won't change their minds even if someone comes back from the grave."

Luke 16:19-31

Often people will say, "I'll believe in God if he does this or that. If he makes my mother better, or if I get a good mark in my SATS test, or perhaps if he sent some special sign. Then I'd believe in him."

But what Jesus is saying here is that God has already sent enough proof that he exists. All a person has to do is to read the stuff that Moses wrote (the first five books of the Bible) and then see what the prophets were saying (lots of the rest of the Bible). That's all the proof anyone could possibly need.

Then in a clever way he talks about someone coming back to life again. People who don't believe what Moses wrote won't be any more convinced if someone dies and then comes alive once more. Of course, Jesus himself died and then came back to life. He was saying that people who weren't willing to believe what Moses said would hardly be likely to change their viewpoint even if they saw Jesus alive again after he'd died. And he was right. Because the sad thing is that even though Jesus has come back to life again (you can read about it at the end of Matthew, Mark, Luke and John), people *still* won't believe in God.

He did ... and he didn't!

What more does God have to do? If we're not ready for him now, when will we be ready?

Chop or crop?

In the vineyard stood a fig tree. It had been there for three years. The owner went down to have a look at it, to see how it was getting on. To his dismay, yet again there were no figs on it.

"Chop it down and use it for firewood," he said. "Every year for the past three years I've been coming here, but haven't found a single fig. I won't have it standing there absorbing all the goodness from the soil. It's a waste of space."

His gardener spoke softly to him. "Why not give it one more year? I'll dig round the soil and put a good fertiliser on it. Hopefully then it will grow some decent figs. If it doesn't, I'll hack it down as you've requested."

Luke13:6-9

Just before this story, Jesus had been telling those listening to him that they would have to change their ways or they would suffer. There would be no way out. No escape for those who didn't do as he said. This all sounded very drastic and alarming and may have made people panic. To calm them down, Jesus reminded them that God was patient and willing to wait. He would put off judging people until the last possible moment, to give them a chance to change their ways.

9. What's God like?

What do you think God is like? Is he...

Young?   Old?   Male?   Does he like football?

Friendly?   Mean?   Does he like netball?   Female?

The questions could go on and on – probably because there aren't any easy answers. If it were easy to know the answers to these questions, then God wouldn't be that fantastic. At least that's what I think.

Jesus said he knew what God was like.

God is like a landowner, the host at a slap-up meal... and a mean judge

Bet that surprised you, didn't it, the bit about him being like a mean judge? I mean, a landowner or farmer is fair enough. God's probably like them because they work hard and get stuff out of the soil. As for the host at a meal, that may be because he gives good food to people. But the mean judge... Well, the mean judge is probably because, em, perhaps... Could it be because...?

God's not fair!

The owner of a vineyard woke up early and, while his family were asleep, quietly left the farm.

(At least they were quietly sleeping, *before* the cockerel woke them all up.)

The owner walked down to the centre of town where men were lounging around waiting to see if there was any work for them. A group of them gathered around and he agreed to pay them one denarius if they would work the whole day. They agreed and he sent them off to work in his vineyard.

FACTS

A DENARIUS WAS A UNIT OF MONEY WORTH ABOUT TEN ASSES. THESE WEREN'T DONKEYS BUT ANOTHER TYPE OF MONEY. IT WAS THE WAGE AN UNSKILLED WORKER WAS PAID FOR A DAY'S WORK.

About three hours later the owner realised that he was going to need even more people to help him out, so he went back to the town to see if there was anybody else who wanted to work.

Sure enough there were some men just hanging around doing nothing. He hired them on the spot and promised that he would pay them a fair wage.

The same thing happened.

The same thing happened.

Back he went once again and saw still more men. They'd been doing nothing all day, for the simple reason that no one had hired them. So the owner agreed to pay them if they went and worked in his vineyard.

At the end of the day, the owner had a word with his foreman. He told him to pay everyone their wages. But he had to start with the people who had been taken on last of all.

The foreman gave these last workers one denarius each. The people who had been hired first thing in the morning saw this and began to get excited. "If that's what they get for just a short period of work, then imagine how much we'll be getting!" they said to each other.

So, when they came to the foreman and held out their hands for their pay, imagine how disappointed they were when they were given a denarius as well. Straight away they went up to the vineyard's owner and began to complain.

"What's the meaning of this?" they shouted. "Those blokes who were working for one measly hour get a denarius and so do we, yet we've been slogging our guts out all day under this boiling sun. It's not fair!"

The owner smiled and said, "My friends, how am I being unfair to you? When we spoke in town at the beginning of the day, you agreed to work for one denarius. That's exactly what I've given you. Off you go with your wage. I've decided to give the men I took on last of all as much as I've given to you. It's my money after all, and I can do what I like with it. Are you cross simply because I've chosen to be generous?"

PARABULZ

I have to let you in on a secret here. This is my favourite parable. Why? I think it's because it's got two great ideas in it. One is that God is generous. He is kind and gives way out of proportion to all expectations. That's a great thing to know about God. The other reason is that there is a bit of a Gotcha in the story too. I bet that as you read it, you thought a bit like the men who complained. Surely it can't be fair that someone who has just worked an hour would get the same as someone who's been there for 12, can it? (Notice that you don't hear the one-hour people complain!)

Welcome to God's world!

He just turns a lot of our thinking upside down

Matthew 20:1–16

Slap-up feast

Do you remember Jesus told us not to grab the best seats at a meal? When he told that parable, one of those listening to him remarked that anybody who ate a meal with God would be a very fortunate person.

A man was getting ready for a really big slap-up meal. He'd got the best caterers to rustle up the most exquisite food ever. There were entertainers, a band, gifts, singing – you name it, he arranged it. The party was going to be the most talked about event in the history of the world.

Everything was in place so he asked his servant to go and round up all the people who had been invited. So off the servant went.

The first man he came to couldn't come.

"I've just bought some land and I need to go and have a look at it."

Nor could the second man.

"I've just bought some top-class ploughing cows and I need to give them a dry run. Sorry I won't be there."

As for the third man:

"I've just got married so I won't be able to make it."

And so it went on. Fed up, the servant went back and told everything to his master.

"One of them had just married a cow, another has bought a wife, somebody else wants to try out their field. No, wait a minute, somebody's about to get married in the middle of a field, one bloke wants to try out his wife and somebody else wants to go and see a cow about something."

The host wasn't very impressed. "Look all over the place. Bring in whoever you can find. I don't mind who they are. In fact, get those people who wouldn't normally have a chance to come to this sort of event... those who haven't got much money, the disabled, the blind, those who have difficulty walking."

So the servant raced off and found as many of these people that he could. He brought them back and sat them down at the table. But there were still empty places.

When he told the host this, his master made him go out once again.

"Go out into the countryside. Look for people everywhere. I want my house to be full with the sound of happiness and laughter. But I promise you one thing. Not a single one of those who were on my original list will get so much as a crumb from the leftovers."

This parable shows us that God is warm-hearted and generous, and is willing to include anyone and everyone in his guest list. It also says that guests should take up the invitation or they will lose out big time.

Invitation

God invites the reader
of PARABULZ
to the
BEST MEAL EVER...
RSVP

Luke 14:15–24

(There is also a slightly different version of this in Matthew 22:1–14, where Jesus warns everyone not to turn up at the party without thinking hard about being ready.)

Is God a meanie?

In a town, whose name I won't tell you because you'll all think it is a dreadful place, there was a judge. His job was to make wise decisions about what was right and wrong. Unfortunately for the town, he was a nasty bit of work. He had no interest whatsoever in what God thought and he certainly didn't care about anyone in the town. The only person he cared about was himself.

In the same town was a lady. Her husband had died and nobody took any interest in the poor old widow. She was in difficulty because one of her husband's enemies was trying to get her. The only hope she had of ever getting rid of him was to ask the judge for help.

But whenever she went to see him, he refused to see her.

Every visit she made she came away with nothing. But she still kept coming with the same cry for help.

Finally the judge had had enough. "I couldn't care less about God or what the people of this rotten town think, but I've had it up to here with this woman annoying me with her nagging and crying. The only way to get rid of her is to see that she gets a fair deal."

WHAT DID THE JUDGE SAY TO THE DENTIST?
PULL OUT THE TOOTH, THE WHOLE TOOTH AND NOTHING BUT THE TOOTH!

Jesus went on to tell his followers that they should buck up and listen to what the judge had to say. Why? Because God will make sure his friends get what is fair. If they keep asking him, he will make sure they get it.

So what's the point about God being like the mean judge?

Well, the only reason the mean judge did anything was because he was being pestered by the woman. (And I'm sure we all know about how to get what we want by pestering.) He didn't care about her or about all the things he was supposed to do for people like her. He just wanted a quiet life.

Now, God is like a judge but he *does* care about people, he *does* care about what is fair and he *does* look after the people who follow him. So, the point is, if even a miserable judge will give a defenceless widow what she wants simply because she never gives up, won't a kind, caring God make sure his people get what is right?

Of course he will.

Luke 18:1-8

10. Mainly about Jesus

Just two more parables to go! Both of them are ones that Jesus told about himself. One of them is about the owner of a vineyard. It's obvious that Jesus liked telling stories about vineyards – which shouldn't come as a surprise. On one occasion he was at a wedding, and when he found out there was no wine left he transformed some water into really tasty wine. (He also told a few parables about weddings too – so I guess he liked those as well!)

WHAT DID THE GRAPE DO WHEN IT WAS SQUASHED?
GAVE OUT A LITTLE WINE.

Another thing is that the Jews thought of themselves as a vineyard that had been planted by God on the earth. So when Jesus talked about vineyards, a lot of the people would immediately think Jesus was talking about the Jewish nation.

See if you think Jesus was in this story.

Vineyard owner goes away

A man owned some land and decided to plant a vineyard. He spared no expense in looking after it. He built a wall all the way round it to keep it safe from thieves and vandals. He dug a space for a winepress inside so that when the grapes were harvested he could squash them on site and make the wine there. Lastly, he built a guard tower overlooking it. Someone could be stationed there to make sure everything was going OK.

Having done all that he decided that rather than look after everything himself, he was going to rent out the vineyard to some tenants who would look after it on his behalf. Satisfied that everything was under control, he went on a long holiday.

Later that same year, at harvest time, he realised that it was time to go and check on his vines and collect some of the grapes. So he sent some of his servants to visit the vineyard.

Instead of greeting the servants and giving them any of the fruit, the tenants treated them dreadfully. They killed one, beat up another and threw stones at another one. Undeterred, the owner sent another lot of servants to fetch what belonged to him. But they were treated in exactly the same way. Those who survived limped back to their master to tell him how they had been attacked by the tenants.

The man thought that he would give it one last go, so he decided to send his son. After all, he thought, they'll treat *him* properly.

But he was wrong. As soon as the tenants saw him approach they quickly held a meeting.

"It's the owner's son!" they said. "If we kill him then the vineyard will become ours."

As soon as the son greeted them, they attacked him, chucked him out of the vineyard and killed him.

It was a dramatic story, but Jesus wasn't quite finished.

"What do you think," he asked those listening to him, "the owner of the vineyard will do to those tenants?"

It's obvious really. He'll give them what they deserve. He'll come and take back what is his, killing all of those bad tenants. Then he'll give the vineyard to other tenants – people who will be responsible and give him what is his.

I wonder what you would do if you had heard Jesus tell that parable?

Would you:

(a)   decide never to rent a vineyard

(b)   give up drinking wine

(c)   a and b

There were some people who did neither of these things. Instead they decided to kill Jesus. Why would they kill him just for telling a parable or two?

The reason is that when Jesus had finished this parable, he left the listeners in no doubt that he looked upon himself as the son of the vineyard owner. Or, as the Jews would have understood it, the son of God himself. He was saying that the Jews had done nothing but treat God's servants badly. He meant God's messengers or prophets who, over the centuries, had told God's message. But most of the time people had not listened.

Now God was giving them one last chance by sending Jesus. If they didn't treat him properly then God would give everything that he'd given to them to other people who would behave differently.

The leaders of the Jews didn't like this idea one little bit. They thought Jesus had overstepped the mark and all they could think about was arresting him and killing him. Yet at the same time, they were afraid because the ordinary people loved Jesus and loved what he did and said. So these leaders would have to wait – but their chance to make the parable come true would certainly come.

> Mark 12:1–12,
> Matthew 21:33–46
> and Luke 20:9–19

A word about allegory

> I THINK I'VE GOT AN ALLEGORY

A-TISH-OO!

You may have heard of the word allegory and thought it meant that pollen or house dust made you sneeze. That's an allergy.

Lots of people see Jesus' parables as allegories. An allegory can be a story where the people and the situations they find themselves in have a deeper meaning than you might think at first. In the story above, for example, I've already said that everyone knew that the vineyard stood for God's people, the Israelites (or Jews). Jesus used an idea that he knew would already mean something to the people he was talking to so that the story would really strike home.

The tricky thing is working out whether every single word, person, place or action has some deep meaning or whether Jesus is just giving his story a bit of extra colour to keep the sleepy ones awake. The best way to work it out is to think why Jesus is telling the parable. Most of the things he taught were meant to make people curious and want to find out more, but I don't believe he'd have made his parables so complicated that you'd have try to work out what every single detail meant. So just read them and enjoy them for what they are – cracking stories with a simple message to really make people sit up and think.

Relocation, relocation, relocation

The final parable in this book is actually one of the first ones that Jesus told. It was another one about himself. As he told it, he had particular people in mind – you and me and everyone who was listening who wanted to follow Jesus.

It comes at the end of the most famous talk ever given. The talk was called the "Sermon on the Mount" for the simple reason that that's where Jesus was. On a mountain. Not the sort with snow on top with ski lifts and Alpine yodellers. More of a big hill really. Perhaps it's called a mount to show that it was a small mountain.

A clever man wanted to build a house. So he drew up plans for his dream home. Then he needed to find a suitable location. After searching hard he found a beautiful spot. He checked thoroughly to see what the ground was like underneath. It turned out to be rock, tough and firm.

In no time at all the house was finished and he was able to move in with his family. He made it just in time, because soon afterwards there was a dreadful storm. The rain bucketed down, the ground was covered in water and the streams burst their banks. The water lapped against the walls of the house, but the man and his family were safe inside. The house coped with everything that the weather threw at it because it had been built on a hard rock.

At the same time a not-so-clever man also decided that he would like to build a house. Like the other man, he drew up plans and then searched high and low for a lovely spot to build it. At last he found what he wanted – right on the seashore. Miles and miles of golden sand stretched as far as the eye could see. It was the perfect place.

In record time his house was up and, together with his wife and children, he moved in. The same storm hit him, too. It poured and poured and the rain lashed against the windows. Suddenly, they noticed that water was creeping inside. Soon they began to hear creaks and groans. It seemed as though the

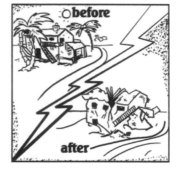

house was moving. Then without warning, the walls caved in, the roof fell and the whole building crashed to the ground. The water had shifted the sand and it wasn't strong enough to support the frame.

There are two types of people in the world, Jesus was saying.

1   People who listen to what he has to say and then live their lives using his words as their guide. When all sorts of difficulties and troubles come along they will be all right.

2   People who listen to what Jesus has to say and then live their lives doing things their own way. When the same difficulties and troubles come along they'll be in a mess.

The first group Jesus calls clever.

The second group are the not-so-clever ones.   Matthew 7:24–27

Finally, are you sitting comfortably...?

Joe and his sister Keri had wanted to see it for ages. They'd never seen it when it first came out. Everyone said it was brilliant. A sort of *The Princess Shrek of the Star Wars Rings Diaries*. Simply the best film ever.

It was their dream come true to get the director's cut gold-plated platinum edition with extra footage.

"Let's watch the additional extras first!" suggested Joe.

There wasn't a lot of time to sit down and watch the whole film until the weekend, but they could snatch a few minutes here and there between homework, football and shopping.

Joe said the fight scenes were mind-blowing. Keri thought they were OK, but what she really loved were the romance bits. When they came on, she cried her eyes out while Joe made puking sounds from behind a cushion. All he wanted to see were the action scenes. So, while Keri was out with her friends, Joe saw Thrambestigoid get his head cut off in slow motion eight times, normal speed four times and fast twice.

At last the weekend came and they had all the time in the world to sit through three and a half hours of blood, snogs, intergalactic conquest and intrigue.

"Come on, Joe. Let's see the whole film," said Keri.

Joe pulled a face. He'd watched all the extra bits so many times, he decided he knew what it was all about.

"No thanks. I must have seen the best bits anyhow," he said. "I can watch those whenever I like, whenever I've got a moment to spare."

"But don't you want to know what the words on the moon tower mean? And don't you want to know who the hooded priest really is? And—"

But he'd gone.

Don't be like Joe!

10 Rulz by Andrew Bianchi

Enjoyed *Parabulz*? You'll want to read *10 Rulz*, also by Andrew Bianchi.

What are the Ten Commandments? And did people in the Bible obey them? A humorous look at some rather naughty Bible characters plus a glimpse at those who obeyed God with their whole heart!

£4.99

God Made Snot by Matt Campbell

A gloopy book of facts about snot: where it's from, why we have it and what God's got to do with it!

£4.99

Snapshots

Snapshots helps 8 to 11s read the Bible for themselves to hear from God – full of prayer and action suggestions, puzzles and challenges.

£3.00 every quarter

Massive Prayer Adventure by Sarah Mayers

A personalised prayer scrapbook to help you get started on the adventure of talking and listening to God.

£4.99

So, who is God? by Robert Willoughby

So, who is God? is no ordinary Bible information book. It uses the Bible to help you find answers to the real questions about God that children ask. These answers are laid out and illustrated in a way that makes you want to read on to find out more!

£9.99

All prices correct at the time of going to print.
All these are available from good local Christian bookshops or SU Mail Order:
Scripture Union Mail Order, PO Box 5148, Milton Keynes MLO, MK2 2YX
Tel: 0845 07 06 006 Fax: 01908 856020 Web: www.scriptureunion.org.uk